# AMMA

**Perumal Murugan** is the author of eleven novels, five collections of short stories, five anthologies of poetry and a collection of personal essays in Tamil. Three of his novels translated into English—*Poonachi, Or the Story of a Goat, Trial by Silence* and *A Lonely Harvest*—were shortlisted for the JCB Prize for Literature in 2018 and 2019. His other novels translated into English include *Seasons of the Palm*, shortlisted for the Kiriyama Prize in 2005, *Pyre*, longlisted for the International Booker Prize 2023, *Current Show* and *One Part Woman*.

**Dr Nandini Murali** is an author, writer, columnist, translator, a communications professional and a gender-diversity professional. She has published both fiction and non-fiction.

**Kavitha Muralidharan** is a bilingual journalist, poet and translator from Tamil Nadu.

TRANSLATED BY
NANDINI MURALI
AND KAVITHA
MURALIDHARAN
AMMA
PERUMAL MURUGAN
eka

eka

First published in Tamil in 2019 as *Thondra Thunai* by Kalachuvadu Publications Private Limited

First published in English as *Amma* in 2019 by Eka, an imprint of Westland Publications Private Limited

Published in English as *Amma* in 2023 by Eka, an imprint of Westland Books, a division of Nasadiya Technologies Private Limited

No. 269/2B, First Floor, 'Irai Arul', Vimalraj Street, Nethaji Nagar, Alapakkam Main Road, Maduravoyal, Chennai 600095

Westland, the Westland logo, Eka and the Eka logo are the trademarks of Nasadiya Technologies Private Limited, or its affiliates.



ISBN: 9789357764803

10 9 8 7 6 5 4 3 2 1



Typeset in Ehrhardt MT Std by Jojy Philip, New Delhi 110 015
Printed at Saurabh Printers Pvt. Ltd.

*For Amma's loved ones, her granddaughters and grandsons:*
*Elamathi, Elankathir, Elampirai and Elamparithi.*

# CONTENTS

# I Breathe through Amma's Heart

(Preface to the original Tamil edition of *Thondra Thunai*, published in July 2019)

I was forty-six the year Amma died. Even today, I inhabit the world she created in those forty-six years with me. A comfortable, beautiful and joyous world. Every attempt I make to leave this world fails; I always return to wrap myself in the mundhanai of Amma's sari. In some sense, the world is like a shell to this snail.

On my education, vocation and my views, I drew away from Amma's world. But I continue to follow what she taught me on matters of my thought, action and way of life. Sometimes I wonder if it is proper that I speak through Amma's words, work through her hands, think through her mind and breathe through her heart. Is this good? I don't know. But habits formed in the cradle will follow one to the cremation ground.

Amma took this shy, introverted child by the hand and pushed him out into the world. The natural ease that I felt when talking to her and being around her has eluded me in every other relationship. There is no need to elevate this as some special kind of love. We fought often, and tantrums were common enough. But none of it ever wedged open a rift.

Like so many people, I too carry the regret that I should have taken better care of her, that I should have kept her happier, in gratitude for all that she had done for me. I will never be free of this remorse.

My mother was the very embodiment of a woman from a farming family. She did not know much beyond her work, her labour. Amma handled all sorts of tasks usually considered the domain of men. She didn't think of work as belonging to men or women. What she did care about was ensuring that her family led a life of dignity, holding their heads high. All her distress and worries were about her family.

Ours was a small family, but we troubled Amma enormously. She was strong, with a force of character that should have earned her a better life, more illustrious, filled with more joy. I console myself that her potential for greatness was limited by her circumstances. Although I do not subscribe to conventional ideas about the institution of family, Amma's view of it has become etched in my being and has made a family-loving man of me.

Though this is a book about my mother, it is not a biography. These essays dwell on various moments from the vast expanse of my memories of her. I wrote two of them when Amma passed away. 'Thondra Thunai', or Invisible Companionship, published in *Kalachuvadu* magazine, and 'Kaatruveli Payanam', or A Journey Along the Path of the Wind, published in *Uyirezhuthu* magazine, were both well received. It is a little disconcerting that obituaries should receive praise. But the joy of planting her in many a heart helped me set this discomfort aside.

After reading 'Thondra Thunai', my son said, 'I didn't feel like crying even when Aaya passed away, Appa. But I wept on reading this essay.' I learnt then that writing was an outlet not only for me. Ambai shared her poignant thoughts on the two essays and also translated them into English. That helped my mother reach a wider readership. My friend Kannan, the publisher of Kalachuvadu Publications, urged me to write this book because he felt that there was an interest among readers, especially given the vital influence my mother has on my writings and in my conversations.

I am grateful to Mu. Vijayakumar, who touched up an old photograph of my mother's for the cover and made it look new, to Rohini Mani, who sought to understand our village before illustrating the cover, and all the others who helped shape this book.

I wrote more than half this book during a writers residency hosted by Art Omi in New York in September 2018. While writing, I read out the essays to my wife, daughter and son every now and then. They were moved by stories about Amma they were already familiar with and surprised by those that were new to them. Their approval gave me confidence.

When I asked my wife Ezhil to write the foreword, she agreed enthusiastically. I am thrilled that she has shared her own memories of Amma, and brought to bear her insight on the essays. There cannot be a more appropriate foreword. It is common enough for a mother to be praised by her son. But is it not rare that a mother-in-law is so admired by her daughter-in-law?

Perumal Murugan<br>
1 May 2019<br>
Namakkal

# Athai-amma

(Foreword to the original Tamil edition of *Thondra Thunai*, published in July 2019)

Before our marriage, I visited Murugu's house once. Contrary to my expectations, his mother went about her work like a young woman and was always on her toes. Murugu and I got married a year later. Ours was a love marriage and an inter-caste marriage. Athai disagreed with her son on this matter, because of which she looked a little exhausted. Yet, without betraying any animosity, she went about her work and took care of us.

She practised rain-fed agriculture and raised a buffalo and a few goats. And we shared the household chores. Athai was not your average mother-in-law—she worked alongside me, helping me wash the dishes or grind the batter.

Ever since I moved into this home after my marriage, I have felt a deep sense of liberation. The first freedom I experienced was from superstitions regarding menstruation. The agrarian life had no place for such beliefs. It is rare to see a woman who does not observe superstitions such as isolation during menstruation or taboos on sexual union or caste. The women of the house usually use these issues to exert dominance. I was taken aback that Athai paid no heed to such things.

The second freedom was from religious beliefs. There was no prayer room in our house. Athai, like me, was not very religious. She would often say, 'A good mind and a clean body are more than enough. After a shower and a prayer offered in god's direction, one can even eat the previous day's rice.' On some days, she offered her prayers to the sun. In these parts, people flock to the temples on new moon days. But I was under no such compulsion in our house.

When there are no such obligations in her in-law's home, a newly married woman feels liberated. Athai alone was responsible for this freedom I savoured. If she had forced me to follow a certain norm, I wouldn't have been able to say no. It is safe to say that she did not believe in superstitions. Sometimes, I waited for Murugu to come home before I had my dinner. She would tease me about this, saying, 'He will eat when he comes. You should have your dinner.'

Athai never set aside any work as someone else's responsibility, no matter what it was. She was always the first to take on any work that needed to be done. Although I was her daughter-in-law, instead of instructing me on a task, she would do it herself. She never looked tired or clammy from working. No matter how much work she did, Athai always looked fresh, as if she were relaxing—a feat I can never achieve because I sweat a lot.

She never palmed off work to the children either, and instead took care of all their needs as well. If I wanted something when I was occupied with some work, Athai would say, 'Stay put, I'll bring it to you,' and rush to get it before I could even get up—a luxury I don't enjoy at my mother's even today.

I grew up being ordered around and reprimanded a lot. No daughter-in-law would dare to remain seated in front of her or expect her to run an errand for them. If perchance my mother had to take on a task, much unpleasantness would follow: she would scream as if a mountain had collapsed on her, and nobody would escape her wrath. She had a knack for getting others to do her work even as she sat in one place—bring me some water, hand me the fan, is something on the stove burning, turn it off, or turn it on. If we refused, she would hit us with the handfan till it broke, all the while keeping up an ear-splitting tirade. Even if we were out playing or doing some other work, she would exercise her authority, ordering us to run errands for her. Having grown up in this environment, Athai's unusual outlook was a big deal for me.

Athai could connect with the emotions of the younger generation. She loved learning new things—new cuisines or using new appliances—and she liked discussing contemporary films. But she was not conceited about her abilities. Nor did she put down others for their inadequacies. I did not know how to do many of the things that she did—investing in monthly chit schemes, swimming, playing cards. But she never snubbed me or bragged about herself.

She patiently explained to us the things we did not know. In the months after Murugu and I got married, Athai taught me everything from cooking to daily customs. If she was unhappy about something, she expressed it in a few words. Even those I did not understand as I barely followed her dialect. Though she felt distant from me and was angry at me, she never nursed any hatred. Only when relatives dropped by were her words to me laced with anger. She did this to appease them. Though I understood the circumstances, I was still weighed down by immense sorrow and helplessness.

No relationship in our home was exalted over the others. Here, I learnt to accept people with their faults and limitations. Athai avoided hurting people and always put herself in others' shoes. Even if an entire village accused a woman, she would look at it from another angle. 'What'll she do,' Athai would say, taking the woman's side.

She did not dig up old quarrels and fan its flames, and made people understand in her own way that they had to move on. That is how she dealt with my impulsive anger too. Once, when my son refused to attend a summer camp, I hit him. Athai placed herself between us to stop me. In trying to dodge her, I pushed her. It was not just her that I was angry with—my built-up anger at not being able to avail of any leaves from the self-financing college I worked in, and at Murugu for letting things be as they were even as he moved out of the village for his job, exploded at once. Athai stumbled and fell down. That was the only time I saw her temper rise.

She let that too pass, considering the circumstances. My son, though, did not get over this incident for years and constantly reminded me of it. But Athai never blamed me after that day, not once. I learnt from her to stop and reflect whenever I got worked up, and that staying calm was always the best course of action. She helped me understand myself better. Athai exerted a creative energy in everything she did.

When we moved to Namakkal, Athai occasionally visited us. During those visits, though she took good care of us, sometimes fights broke out between the two of us, which often ended in Athai walking off with her bags in a huff.

Sometimes, I would need to visit her the same week. I would set out for her home hesitantly, anxious about what she might say. But she would welcome me warmly as if we had not met in a long time. She always waited outside for me when I was scheduled to arrive by the mini bus that passed through the village at a fixed time. If the mini bus did not pull up near the house, she hailed it loudly. She would say I should have come before the day turned hot. Sitting me down on a chair, she would serve me kuzhambu and greens, downplaying her efforts: 'I just put together something.'

If I stayed the night, she would place my cot under the electric fan and hand me clean blankets. As far as she was concerned, this was not hospitality. She was only helping me—a stranger to village life—feel at home. Hospitality came naturally to her. Her humanity shone through in the fact that she did not see me as her daughter-in-law.

Above all, this was what she said to her neighbours: 'The owner of this house has come.' The house she lived in was bequeathed to Murugu when the family property was divided up. The family had acquired this land when my father-in-law was still alive and long before my marriage. It would not have had a front yard had Athai not bought the small piece of land adjoining the house and expanded the space. It took a special kind of generosity to anoint me the owner of that house.

Athai had a special respect for my education and position. She never sent me to the fields, not even to carry ice apples or palmyra tubers. 'She was educated in Madras, why should she do all this?' she would say, and instead bring the produce herself and offer them to me.

After Athai's death, I learnt that she had spoken of me proudly to others in the village when we bought our own house in Namakkal and shifted there. I drew great comfort from hearing people recount what she had said about me: 'She has worked hard, looking after the children and the house while teaching in a private college.'

Her death has left an unfillable void in our children's lives. I would sometimes vent my frustration with something else on my children and beat them. But Athai did not tire of the children and never lashed out at Murugu either. When Murugu was away, my son slept next to her. Worried that she would leave, he would cling to her legs. Once, she called out to show me how he was wrapped around her. When I asked why she was smiling, Athai delightedly told me that she could not even get up to go to the bathroom.

As soon as my son returned from school, he would carelessly throw his uniform all over the place. We got furious if it fell on us. Once, his trousers landed on Athai's head and we got angry as usual. But when we heard the conversation that followed between grandmother and grandson, we could not help but laugh.

'Aaya! Did you see how precise my throw was?' my son asked her.

Gently removing the trousers from her head as if it were a flower, and brimming with pride, Athai said, 'Yes, kannu!'

She enjoyed interacting with children and showered love on my daughter too. When she was one and a half years old, we left her in Athai's care. Though she was unwell, Athai enjoyed my daughter's pranks and took good care of her. My daughter was born in September. Athai insisted that we enrol her in a school when she turned two and half if she could speak well by then, rather than wait another year. Athai taught my daughter to count in the local dialect, and she could recite from one to hundred fluently when she was still a toddler. Whenever she recited the numbers, Athai would listen carefully to make sure she did not mispronounce the word 'muppathu', Tamil for the number thirty. Athai had heard some kids say 'nupathu' instead, and she did not want her granddaughter to make that mistake.

When my daughter told us how Athai had, towards the end of her life, advised her to always be brave, I was in tears. She would have been proud that both her granddaughters grew up to look like her.

Murugu has vividly described Athai's interactions with us in this book, bringing alive the lessons she imparted. From now on, she will be a companion to many others. When reading these essays, mothers like me cannot help but feel guilty. It makes us wonder if we have actually achieved very much. I have led a largely good life and have not faced a sorrow or a hurdle I could not deal with. Nevertheless, there are moments when I feel exhausted. But Athai was never daunted by any obstacle and she never paused; she was a formative presence in the lives of many.

Without wasting any resources, she made sure that her son received the best possible education. Murugu wrote two essays on his mother soon after she passed away. He often shared his memories of her with us and we assumed that is all he had. I was surprised when he told me he was going to write ten more pieces. I wondered what else he could write. But when he read them out to us as and when he finished them, we realised there was so much we had not known.

Books about people like Athai show us how fascinating life is. This book asserts that a woman does not work to build a foundation only for herself; her life's work is also for others. She achieves a lot even as she goes about her routine chores. This collection does not dwell on the everyday dilemmas of ordinary women, and this is its strength. It is an enduring chronicle of the life of a matriarch from an agrarian family—one who absorbed what was necessary from the urban life, adjusted to her new role in the village and managed to unshackle herself from the travails she was subjected to.

'A Ploughman's Accounts' is an extraordinary depiction of a mother. It is fascinating to learn of the bond between a mother and a son in an agrarian community. The essay portrays Athai going about her work with pleasure, without an iota of self-pity. I read it with delight, laughing out loud in many places. Athai's words are important lessons for the materialistically minded.

At the same time, in 'He Is My Lord', the extent to which she adhered to societal conventions is explored, as is her no-nonsense approach to life. We also witness how she changed her views after being shown that it wasn't necessary to always live by society's norms and expectations. The collection details not only how a mother toiled for her family but also how she was an intellectual inspiration for future generations.

Only a few noble souls create something new as they grapple with life's challenges. These essays sketch the life of one such person. Only Athai could triumph over the torments she experienced and show the world that seeds sprout just the same even when sowed by a widow. She transformed her victory over pain into an important social value.

We also see how mother and son treated each other like friends, without feigned respect; they neither sought to control each other nor compromised when expressing their thoughts.

Although Athai did not support our marriage, she never humiliated us. Nor did we force anything on her. The notion that our personal opinions must not harm others emerged naturally in the course of our lives. Had this not been so, the essay 'A Long Journey' would not have found a place in this collection.

When Murugu read out 'The Shadow that Landed with a Thud' to me, I asked him not to include it. I felt that the essay belittled my father-in-law. What Murugu arrives at in the piece need not necessarily be the truth, I argued. Nevertheless, it is included here and could disappoint women who put their men on a pedestal.

There are many universal threads in the book that the reader would find useful. It is not only about the life of a village woman but also about planning, taking on challenging tasks with passionate engagement, protecting what is bequeathed to us, taking on new challenges, inculcating the value of hard work in children, cultivating friendships, changing according to the times, be it men or women, and loving nature.

Those who lend a helping hand, instead of judging the actions of others, are valuable. A person is not defined by their riches. It is possible to lead a disciplined life, no matter the circumstances, and such persons will be a guiding light for others. Athai-amma will continue to be an invisible companion to her son, her grandchildren, her acquaintances and also to those who read this book.

Ezhilarasi
1 June 2019
Namakkal

1

# An Invitation from the Moon

'You were ten months old then,' is how Amma always began her narration of that incident. Every time we went to the fields, she would point to a spot and say, smiling, 'This is where you were, asleep inside a basket.' I can listen to a story about myself repeatedly, without ever tiring of it.

Apparently, I weighed three and a half kilos at birth, and remained chubby until I was four or five. 'By the time I carried you to and back from a place, my hips would break,' Amma often complained, though her tone would give away her pride.

Amma was the eldest daughter-in-law in a joint family that consisted of her father-in-law, mother-in-law and two brothers-in-law. They had three acres of irrigated land and eight acres of rain-fed land—eleven acres of cultivable land in all. They took care of over fifty goats, seven to eight cows, two neighbourhood dogs and their own dog. A boy was employed to take care of the livestock.

Labourers who came to work in the fields had to be served food, and there were at least ten of them every day. Amma handled all the cooking. The entire burden of the kitchen fell on the barely fifteen- or sixteen-year-old girl. Millets and cold ragi porridge was staple food; for the former, pearl millets had to be pounded into rice-like grains and for the latter, finger millets had to be ground to a paste. Even though her mother-in-law and brothers-in-law lent a hand, the kitchen occupied Amma all day. A few years rolled past like this.

Once my two uncles too got married, the three sons and their families moved out to lead their own independent lives. A family house in the village was given to the eldest son and each of the three sons got an acre of irrigated land and two acres of rain-fed field.

Appa's full-time occupation used to be selling sodas and 'colours', or soft drinks, at the market. After the division of the family property, he had to do part-time agricultural work as well. But he could be seen in the fields only on days the market was closed. Since ragi was the staple food, finger millet was the main crop in our acre of irrigated land.

Other crops like cotton, or vegetables like cucumber and ladies' fingers were grown in the interim period. Appa's only responsibility was irrigation. But he constantly drank toddy when he was out in the fields and often passed out. My mother did not allow him to draw water from the well when he was drunk; he made a habit of disobeying her. Amma's work and responsibilities increased manifold after moving out of the joint family.

Around this time, her eldest son—my brother—was five years old, and I was only ten months. Between grazing the cattle, farming and cooking, Amma hardly got a break. Her parents-in-law were not the only ones waiting to see how the daughters-in-law would run their families; the entire village was watching as well. This put pressure on Amma, who worked day and night in a frenzy.

It was the Tamil month of Thai, mid-January to mid-February. Though the millets had been harvested and threshed, the barren millet stalks needed to be pulled out in order to pluck the vegetables from the broad beans and cowpea creepers before they withered away in the sun. These were needed all round the year to make curries, but there wasn't any time to clear the field. While Amma's mother-in-law remarked indirectly, 'The field looks odd. The stalks look like roosters beheaded in a fight,' her father-in-law told her, 'Why don't you hire someone to pull out the stalks, girl?' The incomplete work on the field continued to bother Amma.

Later that night, when she took her elder son who wanted to pee and went outside the house, the moon shone so brightly that it seemed like noon. It was only a couple of days after full moon's day and more than three-fourths of the moon was out. It seemed to be calling out to her with arms wide open. There was a gentle nip in the air. The bright moon banished her sleep and fatigue. She thought she could pull out some of the millet stalks now. Her son was only happy to join her, excited by the idea of playing in the moonlight.

Amma locked up her husband, who lay in a drunken stupor inside the house, hoisted her ten-month-old on to her shoulders, held her five-year-old by hand and left for the fields. She gave the lantern to her oldest. If she walked down the street, the dogs would bark and wake up the neighbours. It would become difficult to answer their questions. She could avoid the dogs if she walked through the field behind the house and went around the residential quarters, even if it added an extra half-mile to what should have been a mile's walk.

There was just one hurdle. There was a dense, thorny patch of the invasive karuvelam tree en route, spread over an area as big as two fields. The narrow path running across it could only fit one person at a time. And on that path, the karuvelam would block the moonlight, with only dappled light filtering in through the leaves. The lantern would come in handy. Amma was scared of snakes more than the darkness.

On the other side was a tar road leading to Erode, flanked on either side by dense tamarind trees. It would take only moments to cross the road, but there was another obstacle. A madman with dreadlocks and clad only in a dirty towel wrapped around his hips was often spotted on this road during the day. He was not known to have hurt anyone, but Amma was worried about encountering him at this time of the night.

After crossing the road, she would be in fields empty after the harvest, and so she had nothing more to worry about. Making her way through these, she would reach the millet field. The toddler weighed her down, while the older son walked enthusiastically on his first moonlit outing.

Once they passed the karuvalem patch and quickly crossed the big road, Amma walked unhurriedly and reached the millet field. There were no troubles on the way, but the weight of the child on her shoulders, speed-walking and fear had made her heart race. Sitting on the bund, she placed the baby on her lap. He was fast asleep. Within sight was a cow shed and next to it a goat pen. There would be drinking water around there. Following his mother's thoughts, the elder son said, 'I'll go fetch water, Amma,' and took off before she could even respond. The boy was intrepid. As she sat watching his silhouette, she saw him reach the shed.

He came back in some time with a stray dog in tow. It ran ahead of him wagging its tail and circled Amma's legs.

The boy was balancing a basket taller than him on his back and a pot of water in his hand. To prevent the basket from touching the ground, he was walking slightly bent over. When Amma thundered in anger, 'What is this basket for?' he smiled and said, 'You can place thambi in this, no?' He was a smart kid.

Placing the child in the basket, and leaving the dog and the boy to guard the baby, Amma stepped into the field. She said a prayer and began to pull out the stalks. Since they were already turning brown, and there was dew to aid the process, the stalks came out easily. Her son and the dog ran around in the bunds and the furrows emptied of millet stalks. She wondered if the baby would wake up with all the noise and kept an eye on the basket as she worked.

The roots looked like tightly knotted hair buns as they came away, gently like a flower, when she tugged. She left behind a few stalks for the broad beans and cow pea creepers to latch on to. A little quail that had built its nest among the creepers got startled and flew away. The eggs and little chicks left behind would attract snakes. Though Amma was not afraid of snakes, she was worried about stepping on a well-fed, immobile one, which would then bite her.

The moon lit up the furrows now that the stalks were harvested. Amma was neither tired nor aware of the passing of time. Only when her hands found no more stalks did she look up and realise that she had cleared the entire field.

Anxious about having ignored her sons, she rushed to the basket and found her baby asleep, just as she had left him. Her elder son was asleep beside the basket, next to the dog that was sleeping with its head tucked into its curled-up body. It was the first to wake up, stretching and wagging its tail.

Lifting the baby on to her shoulders again, Amma took the basket and the dog back to the cowshed. The trio reached home just as dawn was breaking.

Amma always concluded this story with three observations.

The baby had slept peacefully through the entire thing, without so much as a tiny wail. He was such a good child.

The next day, her father-in-law ran back in shock after seeing the empty fields and told his wife, 'An evil spirit has pulled out all the millet stalks in the field overnight!' Unfazed, his wife said, 'All right. We have been spared the work.'

The husband, passed out drunk from a purudu* of toddy and locked up in the house, had been unable to get out. He had to take a leak in a corner inside. Getting rid of that stench became the greater challenge for Amma.

---

* Purudu is derived from purudai, the native variety of bottle gourd, which was hollowed out, dried and used as a container for toddy.

2

# The Story of the Intestine Meat

Amma did not allow cooking to take up all her attention or time. The stove would burn as she went about feeding the cows and goats. She could do multiple tasks at once and it was hard to tell which of them was the most important. What seemed like an additional task to an onlooker could actually be the most pressing one. And cooking was never an all-consuming task for her.

She largely cooked with firewood that emitted only a little smoke. There were palm or coconut sheaths to light the stove. You could use palm fronds too, but they burn out quickly. So Amma only used the sheaths. She always came back home with a couple of them, adding to her endless supply. After lighting the stove, she chose pieces of firewood that would burn longer, and stacked them so that air could pass through. To keep the fire going, she only had to slightly nudge the wood as she passed by. Embers from the long-lasting firewood would fall inside the stove and keep it warm even when the fire went out.

Amma would soak rice in the right amount of water, place it on the stove and add a couple of pieces of firewood. She then covered the vessel with a plate, kept a blowpipe on it and left to attend to other tasks. When the rice boiled over, the weight of the pipe would keep the lid in place. Every now and then, she would lift up the lid a little to let in some air, and that would settle the boiling rice. By the time the fire went out, the rice would be cooked. It would continue to soften in the heat of the embers, soaking up the remaining water, and there would be no need to drain the starch. Amma would let the cooked rice sit on the stove while she finished her other chores.

She also made porridge, millet rice and even curries, in this unique manner of cooking with embers. Amma would mash the lentils, add vegetables, place the dish on the stove, add the firewood and that was it. The vegetables would cook in the fire from the wood and then in the heat from the embers. She did not have to hover around and tend to the pot.

Amma's cooking was simple. She hardly used any spices apart from chillies to flavour her curries. Quite frequently, she made kadaisal with mashed vegetables and lentils. When she made a poriyal of sautéed vegetables, it would double up as curry, to be mixed and eaten with rice. She took care to pair different kinds of rice with the right kind of curry: Pearl millets served with paruppu kuzhambu, or mashed and seasoned lentils, and kootu, or boiled and seasoned vegetables, was delicious. Millets porridge was only served with broad beans, or mashed greens such as pannai or kumitti. The rice of paddy paired well with all curries, but shallots were an essential ingredient in any curry. Amma could coax shallots to yield different flavour profiles.

Some vegetables are meant to be sautéed while others ought to be curried. Ladies' fingers should not be cooked with lentils but curried separately. There is no such thing as broad beans sambar; the vegetable is best sautéed. Mashed lentils should be spiced with red chilies, not green. Coconut should be used only in certain dishes—it is an important addition to the greens of sunberry, should be ground when added to meat curries eaten with idlis and dosais, and is to be strictly avoided if the curry is meant for rice. Cooking is possible without groundnut oil or gingelly oil but not without castor oil. Two drops of it must be added when lentils are boiled, and only castor oil can be used to sauté shallots. Amma invented her own little cooking rules.

She was also precise with the amount of food she cooked. There were no leftovers and the curry she made lasted just one meal. We were always left asking for more. To avoid wasting even the curry stuck to the vessel, Amma would put some rice inside, mix it up with the dregs and feed us each a handful of this. It tasted like heavenly amudham. We finished Amma's food by wiping the vessel clean and licking the last of it off our fingers; there was no other way to eat it. When we were disappointed about not having more to eat, Amma would say with a smile: 'The food will taste good only if there's just enough of it. It'll taste even better if there's a little less.' I apply this, one of Amma's important cooking principles, in all aspects of my life to enhance it.

Our entire family was a slave to Amma's paruppu kuzhambu. My father and elder brother were crazy about it and asked her to make it every day. It was their favourite, even though her other curries, whether of bitter gourd or ladies' fingers or bottle gourd, tasted good as well. No matter who came home, Amma always made paruppu kuzhambu. My brother's children and mine visited her especially to eat it.

Everyone in my family knew how to cook; men from agricultural families usually do. I have watched Amma make her paruppu kuzhambu many times and even got the recipe from her, but I have never been able to recreate the taste of her cooking. The magic was in her hands, what we call kaippakkuvam. Even today, when my wife makes this curry, she asks me: 'Isn't it somewhat like what Athai used to make?' All of us who attempt to make it can only reproduce the flavour 'somewhat'. The best of it was lost with Amma's hands.

Once, when I was visiting Amma, a student of mine—who was then a professor in a private college—came to meet me, and Amma made lunch for us. He later wrote in an essay: 'I have never had such tasty sunberry curry in all my life. Amma had cooked it in a mud pot atop a firewood stove. I can still savour the taste of it deep inside my heart.' She received many such compliments for her culinary skills.

Each of us claims our mother's cooking is the best, perhaps because we grow up eating it. Even today, I think of Amma's cooking whenever I eat. When I see a vegetable, I can't help but wonder how she would have cooked it. Though I like tasting all sorts of dishes—one needs new experiences even with food—it is Amma's cooking that dominates my taste buds and my heart even today.

It would be incomplete to speak of her cooking without narrating this incident:

She had allotted three rows in our farm for our personal use. There, she grew different types of vegetables and creepers, including four or five brinjal plants, two or three ladies' fingers plants, a bottle gourd creeper and a pumpkin creeper. There were also a couple of cluster bean creepers, which once yielded a bounty of tender beans. Amma brought back a lapful of them for dinner. She chopped them finely, each piece only as long as the lines on the little finger. Then she boiled them and sautéed them with kadalai mizhagu podi, or spiced gram powder.

Amma made two kinds of hand-pounded podis to use in her cooking—kadalai mizhagu podi and ellu mizhagu podi, or spiced sesame powder. I always carried two bottles of these podis with me when I was a college student and lived away from home. Mixed with warm rice, these podis made for a delicious meal. On days I felt lazy, I made do with the podis rather than make a curry. Many of my friends too were in its thrall. Cluster beans sautéed with kadalai mizhagu podi tasted out of this world. We used to call it 'intestine meat' because it was that delicious.

That day, Amma came back home for a break when the sun grew hot. She made a panful of this poriyal before heading back to the field again. Dinner was ready, only rice needed to be cooked. Anna had just come back from school and was hungry. He searched the house but found nothing to snack on. Then he took the lid off the pan on the stove outside and found the cluster beans–intestine meat. He took some on a plate and found it irresistible. He served himself another helping of it, but was left wanting more. One more serving … and another … the pan was wiped clean.

Then Anna got scared. He had eaten all of the cluster beans, what about dinner? Amma would thrash him soundly when she returned. Had he not selfishly finished it on his own, he would be asked. He came to a decision. Because it was on the stove outside, Amma would think a dog had eaten it. After all, only he knew what had happened. He made the necessary arrangements and went out to play.

When Amma returned after nightfall, she found the pan lying face down on the ground. The lid lay scattered on the other side. Griping about a dog having eaten her boys' favourite 'intestine meat', she cooked rice and lentils together for a make-do meal.

'I had tasted it while cooking. It was so good. Did I make it for it to be wasted on a dog? Which dog could have eaten this? Which dog would have been so bold? If I catch hold of it, I'll break its hips.

'I've seen dogs eat rice, but I've never seen a dog gobble up and wipe clean a vessel full of vegetables, that too one cooked with spices! Looks like it couldn't lay its hands on anything else. I wonder how long it had been starving for.

'Maybe because *these* dogs kept calling it intestine meat, perhaps the dog too thought it really was meat.'

And so she rambled. The dogs we raised were only fed one meal a day at night. We cooked either pearl millets or ragi especially for them, mixed it with a little curd or milk and fed them. They rarely got any food during the day, unless they managed to hunt something in the fields. On the days we cooked meat, we fed them the bones and the thinner part of the curry mixed with rice. When ewes or cows gave birth, we fed the placenta to the dogs. Raw placenta takes time to digest, so the dogs would go without food for the next two or three days. They have been trained not to enter the house, or even the porch. They don't touch the food until we serve it to them in a bowl and give the command to 'Eat' or 'Drink'. Our dogs did not steal. The dog that had eaten the food must have come from elsewhere, we assumed.

'Why didn't you leave the food inside? You left it out for the dogs to find and are grumbling now,' my father scolded her.

'I always leave it on the stove. A new dog seems to have emerged from somewhere, somehow, just to eat this.'

The 'dog' that had actually eaten the food was not hungry anymore. Without making this obvious, it put up a pretence of eating a little and went to bed immediately.

In the middle of the night, my brother felt his stomach rumble. He got up and went to the fields to relieve himself. Some time passed and his stomach rumbled again. Noticing that he had made a few trips to the field, Amma realised that he was the 'dog' that had eaten the cluster beans. Though she was always alert even when asleep and the slightest sound would wake her, she continued to lie quietly until it became obvious that Anna's trips to the field weren't about to stop.

'What is it, my kannu? Do you have diarrhoea? What did you eat? Did you eat anything at school?' she sat up and asked.

'No, Amma,' he replied, but didn't elaborate.

Amma lit the stove and made strong black tea for him. After drinking the tea, he ran to the field once more and then finally fell asleep.

Long after dawn, pointing to Anna who was still not awake, Amma said, 'The dog that had eaten the cluster beans is still sleeping.' When he woke up, everyone already knew. Perhaps Amma told everyone because she was proud that her food was irresistible.

Everyone made fun of Anna. News spread through the village and even boys in our school asked him: 'Were the cluster beans that your mother cooked so good? We heard you even ate the vessel.' For a few days after, everybody called him 'sattiyoda thinni'—the one who ate the vessel with the food. Anna was quite embarrassed.

The following week, Amma made the cluster beans–intestine meat again.

'He ate all of it last week. Don't give him even a bite today!' I yelled.

To placate my brother, Amma said, 'We should learn to eat everything in moderation. The tongue has no limit, we should train it,' and served him some cluster beans. Anna refused to eat it or even look at it. Amma tried to get him to eat it, but he did not relent. Appa said he might have developed an aversion for the dish because it had given him such a bad bout of diarrhoea. 'He will eat it again when he feels better,' Appa reasoned. We all ate the cluster beans–intestine meat, poking fun at him throughout the meal.

But Anna refused to eat cluster beans after that too. Amma tried to coax him and even forced him, but in vain. If someone spoke of the incident when Amma made cluster beans, she would say with a sigh: 'Enough, don't talk about that intestine meat story.'

We hoped that my brother would change his mind over time. But he never ate cluster beans ever again in his life.

3

# Making Murukku

The Tamil month of Panguni, mid-march to mid-April, was important for us. There was no work in the fields during this time because the harvesting would have already been done by then and the fodder would have been cut. All that was left was some odd jobs. The bone-dry stubble of the castor plants, called kattai, needed to be uprooted. This was done with a tool called kattai vetti, while the groundnuts were collected with a hoe. Apart from these few tasks in the fields, most of the work at this time was at home.

The groundnuts were sold after some had been set aside for sowing the next season. These had to be shelled, an important task in the month of Panguni, and was called kadalaikkai tholitthal. There are machines to do this now, but back then we had to do it by hand.

We shelled the nuts day and night, without employing help, who had to be paid for every padi, a traditional measure, of nuts shelled. Amma was an expert. Done right, two groundnuts can be shelled simultaneously. The right hand would take a nut to the mouth, the front teeth would crack the shell, then the hand would drop the shell and the nut into the two piles between one's outstretched legs. The hand would quickly return to pick another and take it to the mouth. Simultaneously, the left hand would smash a groundnut on the floor. This was easy if the floor was cement. On a mud floor, we used a small flagstone.

Amma used her left hand with greater ease, and this meant she could simultaneously shell three groundnuts. She would smash on the floor a groundnut each with her right and left hand. In between, she accomplished another task with her left hand—throwing a groundnut towards her mouth. Without fail, she would catch it with her front teeth, break it, and spit the shell and the nut out without using her hands. This is how she shelled three groundnuts in one go. None of us could master this skill, it was Amma's alone.

She put Anna and me to work by enticing us with money and playtime. Amma would place a padi of groundnuts in front of us and tell us we could go play once we had shelled them. On moonlit nights, my grandmother, aunts and all the boys and girls in the family would gather in the sprawling cemented front yard at the home of Chitthappa, or my father's younger brother, carrying our groundnuts in a basket.

We shared stories as we shelled the nuts, and it was the best time for riddles. Even a child from our parts knew the answer to this common riddle: 'It is visible when it blooms, but invisible when it yields fruits. What is this?' Groundnut. The castor plant, grown as an intercrop with the groundnuts, too had a riddle of its own. 'Its surface is covered with thorns, but it is not the jackfruit. Its inside is white, but it is not the coconut. What is it?' Time passed quickly as we entertained each other with these riddles. Work progressed, so did the storytelling. Those were wonderful nights.

We competed to be the fastest to shell our piles. Chitthappa's children and I were young, and so my brother often won. On the rare occasion one of us did, the mood turned celebratory. We would yell, 'Loser, loser,' and join forces to taunt my brother, who would walk away in a huff.

While our attention was on the games, Amma stayed focused on the groundnuts. If it rained during Chitthirai, mid-April to mid-May, farming activities would resume, which means that all the tasks related to the groundnuts must be done before then.

Our nails became discoloured and our fingertips turned red from the incessant shelling. Our lips too were sore and burned. We applied butter at bedtime to soothe our lips. Seesawing between the joys and pains, we would somehow manage to shell all the groundnuts.

After this, the nuts had to be sieved as not all of them were fit for use as seeds. Separating the vatha paruppu, or the dried and shrivelled nuts, from the healthy ones was a tedious job. Since the circular iron sieve used to separate the two was expensive, only a few people in the village had one and it was in great demand during this time. As rent for the sieve, some demanded a vallam, equivalent to four padis, of groundnut seeds. But many others lent it without a fee for the sake of friendship or family. We would borrow the sieve for free, and the process would begin.

It was a Herculean task. Amma sat with her legs outstretched, and the basket of shelled groundnuts by her side. She scooped the nuts from the basket on to the sieve, then holding the sieve between her legs, she shook it forward and backward, upward and downward. The shrivelled nuts passed through the sieve and fell down, leaving behind nuts suitable for seeding. Amma poured these into a basket placed on the other side. This work went on for a few days.

To protect them from ants, the shrivelled nuts and the seeds were tied up in separate sacks. As were the castor seeds. Only two villages in our region had oil extraction mills, both at a distance of five to six miles from our village. The only way to reach them was through the fields and it was impossible to even push a cycle along this path, let alone ride one.

Our home had two oil cans, one for castor oil and one for groundnut oil. Any leftover oil from the previous year was filtered and poured into bottles or into thookkupposis, round metal containers with handles. The cans were then cleaned thoroughly to remove all grease and left to dry in the sun. Amma spread this task out over two or three days.

Tuesdays, Thursdays and Sundays were considered auspicious for oil extraction. The three of us would set off early in the morning on one of these days. There would be a sack on Anna's head and another on mine. Amma carried a basket with an oil can on her head and another basket at her hip. We also took along a thookkuposi with palaya soru, previous day's rice soaked in water, which we took turns carrying.

The bullocks were yoked to the hand press, but the process of oil extraction would begin only after the day grew warmer. By then, we would have reached the mill. There might be sacks that other people had already dropped off the previous day, but Amma would entreat the mill owner to grind our sacks first: We have come a long way and it would be difficult to come again another day, she would plead.

Though there were separate presses for groundnut oil and castor oil, if there was not enough inflow, the same press would be used for both. In which case, we had to return another day for the castor oil as it involved a lot of work and would keep us at the mill all day. The oil needed to be heated and then strained, and we would have to wait until it cooled.

The rice in our thookkuposi and an idli shop in that village took care of our hunger as we waited through the day. Anna and I loved to eat shop-made idlis. The taste of the kuzhambu in shops cannot be recreated at home. 'If you get used to the taste of the shop kuzhambu, the tongue can't be controlled, da,' Amma would scold us.

The most difficult part was bringing home the filled oil cans. Amma would wrap the mouths of the cans with cloth, which she knotted securely. She then placed them in the baskets and swathed them in straw, so they didn't shake on the journey back. While she carried the bigger groundnut oil can, Anna carried the smaller one with castor oil. Since oil cakes were taken as fee for the extraction, we didn't have the additional burden of carrying them too. Any extra oil was poured into the thookkupposi, and if there was still more, it went into small bottles. These were mine to carry.

We had to keep an eye on the road as we walked. Even a slight stumble on a little stone could topple the oil cans. So Amma always walked with care, and constantly warned us to be careful. She remained anxious until we reached home. We had to be back before sunset as it would be tough to walk on the narrow pathways and through the fields at night. Moreover, ghosts, out and about at night, were said to be attracted to the aroma of freshly pressed oils. Amma always carried a bunch of neem leaves and coal in the basket to ward them off. She breathed easy only after we had brought the year's supply of oil home and safely deposited them in their place. Every year, a day was thus set aside for oil.

The freshly pressed oil could not be used right away, and so preparations would begin soon after it was home. Before we could cook with them, we had to light lamps with the oils for the presiding deity of our village, Mariamman, and for our family deity, Kariakaliamman. Anna and I were usually on our summer vacation around this time, so we were free to visit the Mariamman temple any Friday. We also had to choose an auspicious day for the Kariakaliamman temple that was ten miles away. On the chosen day, the four of us would set out for that shrine. Appa and Anna would each ride a cycle, with Amma on Appa's cycle and me on Anna's. After this, Anna and I were put through the ordeal of drinking castor oil as purgative therapy.

A day before this, Amma would have prepared millet rice. When it cooled, she would scoop out handfuls of it, place it in a container and soak it in water. On the day of the therapy, she would wake us early in the morning. She would bring to a boil the water in which the millets had been soaking for a day, fill a fourth of a tall glass with it and the rest with the new castor oil. The oil would melt in the gentle heat, making it easier to drink. Once we had the glass in our hands, we had to close our eyes and gulp it down in one go. Amma then handed us a piece of palm jaggery to check the nausea, and it left a sweet aftertaste too.

We would spend half that day running between our home and the fields. Castor oil washes out the stomach. Before we grew exhausted from the dehydration, Amma would cook paddy rice and bedhi rasam, also known as pacchappuli rasam, made of raw ingredients that were not sautéed or tempered. Though the rasam wasn't usually appetising, on that day it would taste divine. After we ate the rasam and rice, the diarrhoea would gradually cease. This was our sole diet that entire day. If the diarrhoea persisted, a glass of buttermilk would settle the stomach.

But the oil treatment did not end here; its climax was yet to come.

When Amma visited the Tuesday market, we would know right away that she was going to make murukkus. 'Amma! When will you make it?' we would keep pestering her. 'We will, da!' is all she would say, without telling us when.

One day, out of the blue, she would wake me at 3 or 3.30 in the morning. The oil would already be warming on the stove. Amma always used long-burning firewood when making murukkus. The dough too would be ready in a big brass container. We never had the faintest idea when she had soaked the rice, ground it in the mortar and pestle, and kneaded the dough with cumin, carom seeds and other ingredients.

She never woke Anna, who did not have the patience for making murukkus. Amma declared that I was the right assistant for the job, and I was proud of this.

She was an expert in kneading the dough to the right consistency and in frying it. The dough was stuffed into the murukku maker and squeezed out on to the surface of an upturned ladle. There were four to five moulds in the maker. Though each mould was of a different shape, they essentially produced two kinds of murukkus—mul murukku and medhu murukku. Mul murukku with its spiked surface is harder to chew, whereas medhu murukku cracks easily and melts in the mouth.

Amma would slip the discs into the hot oil. My job was to flip these with the tip of an iron handle used to make dosais, keep a check on their consistency and transfer them to a vessel when cooked. Squeezing the dough out of the maker requires a lot of arm strength. It is also difficult to stand by the boiling oil and fry it, as heat waves constantly hit your face. The process requires patience. Amma and I would chitchat as we worked.

After putting out the stove, Amma transferred the fried murukkus into a large moda, already readied for this. I could take a break then, that is, eat some murukkus. By the time they were all made, I would have eaten at least ten murukkus. 'Eat less,' Amma would scold me. When the dough was used up and two modas and another vessel were filled with murukkus, dawn would break.

Throughout the month-long vacation, we would be at it until the containers were empty. 'The two bandicoots have wiped the moda clean,' Amma would tease us and laugh heartily.

# 4

# THE GIFT ACCOUNTS

When I was in class two, our family started keeping an accounting notebook for moyi. We used Anna's class six English notebook for this, because it had many unused pages left at the end of the academic year. We put down two columns with the titles: 'moyi given', cash gifts we had given others and were to get back in the future, and 'moyi to be given', that others had given us and we were obliged to pay back. Since we rarely had any special occasions, the 'moyi given' column was always longer.

Had there been any girl children in our family, there would have been more special occasions to celebrate. But we were both boys. It was customary to celebrate a girl's puberty on a grand scale. She would also have a wedding at the age of sixteen or seventeen. Though we had no such opportunities, there was one special occasion after my parents' wedding—my brother's ear piercing ceremony. Amma had lost her first child soon after it was born. My brother was the first child in our entire extended family and many offerings were promised to god when he was born.

My parents had not handed out invitations even for their wedding. Only the rich could afford them. But invitations were printed for Anna's ear piercing and the whole family was in a celebratory mood. For many years, copies of the one-page invitation to an 'Ear Piercing Ceremony' were lying around at home. Whenever Anna waved it in the air and told me with pride, 'They printed invitations for my ear piercing ceremony, da!' I used to ask Amma, crying, 'Why didn't you print invitations for me?' Amma poked fun at me by way of consolation, 'We'll print invitations for your wedding.'

Though my parents had received moyi for Anna's ear piercing, there was no practice of keeping accounts for the gifts then, nor were there literate people in the village. Amma had made a mental note of all those who had given money and how much they had given. We began maintaining an accounts notebook only ten years after the ear piercing ceremony held in 1963.

That night, by the light of a lantern, the four of us entered the details of all previous moyi transactions. First, we tackled the moyi given, a difficult one. Someone might have given us moyi for Anna's ear piercing and we might have later repaid them during a function at their home. If the parents in that house were old or if it was the last wedding in their family, we would have given them a moyi equivalent to what they had gifted us and the accounts would have been balanced. If the family had two or three children, there could be confusion over which of the children would repay any moyi balance after the parents passed on. Tallying the accounts averted such confusion. Sometimes, family members requested that we gift them the exact amount they had gifted us. If the accounts were balanced, there was no need to make an entry in the notebook.

If there were to be more functions in our home in the future, then we would gift more money than what the family had gifted us. Only the additional amount was to be entered as the moyi given, and which we were entitled to get back. Gifting a large sum would come in handy when it was returned later. If someone had given us five rupees as gift, we would add another five to our gift to them. Then, we would get back five rupees during the next function in our family.

As Amma recalled each transaction from memory, I entered them in the notebook. My handwriting was tiny and rounded, and always within the printed lines. I was taught by my class one teacher that the letters should neither touch the line above nor below. As early as then, my writing was beautiful and legible. Anna split each of his letters, and the lines in a page or the pages in the notebook were never sufficient for him. So he always handed over the task of writing to me.

I put down each person's village name, field name, birth name and nickname in a row. A typical entry read: 'Kattupatti Manakkadu Murugan (Soolayan) = Rs 5.' A person was not always identifiable by their birth name, so I also wrote down their nickname in parentheses. For instance, the people in our village did not know my father's birth name. If an entry were to be made against his name, he would be identified as Kattupatti Masayangounder, using his nickname Masayan.

We somehow managed to complete the entries for the moyi we had given. Those we missed would be added later as and when we remembered them. Next, we tackled the moyi that we had to give, which would include people we were yet to repay after Anna's ear piercing.

For the first entry, Amma said without hesitation, 'Mondhapalayam Murungaikaadu Santhayi: Rs 1.' That was the minimum value of a cash gift then.

Since Mondhapalayam was far from where we lived, we asked Amma who she was. 'A grandmother,' she said, and went on to explain the relationship in a mother's style: 'my mother's uncle's father-in-law's sister's …'. She also added that this debt wouldn't be written off any time soon. Kanthayi paati's son and daughter-in-law had passed away and she only had a grandson, a young boy. Our next chance to repay the moyi would be his wedding. Until then, this would remain a debt.

The 'moyi to be given' column did not take more than a page, while the 'moyi given' column covered five to six pages. After this, we habitually entered the moyi given whenever we attended a function. Entries under 'moyi to be given' were struck off and additions were made under 'moyi given'. After all the pending gift debts were cleared, Kanthayi's name alone remained.

Whenever the notebook came out, we discussed our debt to Kanthayi paati. If we wondered aloud that maybe paati's grandson had got married already, Amma would say confidently, 'Would paati get him married without telling me? She will definitely remember the one rupee she had gifted us. Even when I met her at the market last year, she reminded me that I must attend her grandson's wedding, return the gift and partake of the feast.'

Kanthayi paati did not come for Anna's wedding. Amma told us that she had visited paati in her village and personally handed her the invitation. Paati was anxious about not being able to find a bride for her grandson and she couldn't bring herself to attend any weddings. Apparently, she pulled a long face if she was even invited for one. Since she did not give us any moyi for Anna's wedding, our debt to her remained at a rupee. Even if she had come, she couldn't have given too much. We didn't accept much money during his wedding, because by then we had come to believe that moyi was something of a burden. We only allowed gifts that amounted to what we had already given out as moyi.

Years later, Amma heard through someone that Kanthayi paati's grandson had been married off. People took the moyi accounts quite seriously. If someone forgetfully gave less than what they were obliged to, an argument would ensue: 'We gave you so much, how could you give so little?' Even if one was unable to attend a function, the moyi amount was sent through someone else. If that was not possible, then one would visit the family later, apologise for not attending the celebration and hand over the cash. Sometimes, family members would visit those who hadn't attended to collect the money. Moyi helped families cope with the expenses of a function at home and there were rules that had to be followed.

Amma was offended that she had not been invited to the wedding of Kanthayi paati's grandson. She also had a debt to clear. In the twenty years since we had received that one rupee, its value had reduced to nothing. But a debt is still a debt, no matter its value. 'How did the old woman forget to invite me?' Amma asked, frustrated. But she didn't leave it at that.

On a day my school was closed, Amma finished her work early in the morning and we took a bus to Mondhapalayam. We had no other relatives there. Paati, her grandson and his new bride were at home, amidst the fields. Paati was now so old that she had to use a walking stick. They practised rain-fed agriculture but seemed to have five to six acres of land.

Amma came close to fighting with Kanthayi paati over not being invited to the wedding. Paati said apologetically that she had sent word through her grandson and assumed he would have invited us. By way of pacifying Amma, the grandson added that there had been a lot of people to invite, and so he must have lost track, and that it was only an oversight.

Even as they were talking, Kanthayi paati asked her grandson's wife to cook for us. Though Amma tried many excuses, such as the goats and cows needed to be tended to, the old woman would have none of it. 'The meal will be ready as we talk. She's like my granddaughter and is very efficient,' she insisted. Tender coconut water from their trees was served. Paati and Amma chatted endlessly. I roamed the fields with her grandson, an elder brother to me. We had paruppu kuzhambu and spicy vadais for lunch.

Paati pressed Amma to stay back: 'You have come here after so long. I don't know how much longer I'll be alive.' But once Amma started thinking about work, she wouldn't stay a minute longer.

When taking leave, Amma drew out a five rupee note from her bag and handed it over to Kanthayi paati. But the old woman refused to accept it. 'Isn't it just a rupee?' she asked with a toothless grin.

'Yes. But of what value is a rupee today? Please take the five rupees,' Amma said, still holding out the note.

Paati was stubborn. 'We forgot to invite you this time. Do you think he will keep in touch after I am gone? If I die with a debt to you, will I attain salvation? Just give me a rupee.' She wouldn't listen to reason and only accepted the rupee.

'Thank god! The debt is finally cleared,' Amma said in relief on our way home. Later that night, we struck off Kanthayi paati's name from the 'moyi to be given' category. The account was closed.

5

# The Shadow that Landed with a Thud

Appa visited the Palani temple every month on the day of the Krithikai star without fail and prayed to Lord Murugan for a second child. Because I was born from the god's blessings, I was named Murugan. Appa showered love on me when I was a baby, but he started disliking me when I became a little boy.

But he adored my elder brother. Appa carried him on his shoulders until my brother was seven or eight years old. He took Anna along everywhere he went and Anna too followed him around like a puppy. Appa ignored me, though. I would run behind him, crying, only for him to yell, 'Go back home!' and push me away.

Whenever he brought home something to eat, he gave it to my brother. He didn't hand me the packet of snacks even once. I would get a share only if Anna chose to give me some. Or, Amma had to fight for my due. I didn't get anything without crying for it first. Sometimes, my brother ran away with the packet and I got nothing.

The two of us had strikingly contrasting personalities. My brother was brave. He jumped into wells, climbed palm and coconut trees with his chest upright, yoked the fiercest of bulls, rode bullock carts, irrigated the fields and ran around fearlessly in the night. Like my father, he could do hard physical labour. He was an extrovert and easily picked up quarrels. He was always complimented by someone or the other for being a 'live wire'.

I had none of these talents. For starters, I was a coward. I had to work hard to learn even the simplest of physical tasks from my mother. And I was always hesitant and unsure of myself. I ran and hid if there was a group of four people. I preferred solitude. Books and writing kept me company, and these became my world from when I was very young. I have often wondered if my father disliked me because my personality was so different from his. Do parents accept their children only if they have the qualities they desire? Is it the practice to push away the child who lags behind?

It's not just that my father didn't like me, he also never missed an opportunity to humiliate me. He called me 'pombalachatti', a transgender, because I was often seen holding on to my mother's sari and because I played with girls. Amma consoled me that Appa had said unintentionally and only once that 'A pombalachatti has been born in my house,' and others had caught on to the term. If someone wanted to bug me, they called me 'pombalachatti' and 'pottaiyan', or effeminate. Though I didn't quite know the meaning of these words, I reacted to them strongly because I sensed that they were meant to insult me. I threw stones and whatever else I could get hold of at everyone who teased me. On such occasions, I have often heard Amma scold Appa, 'How can we even question others, if the father treats his son like this?'

Appa also gave me the name 'eruvukali', one who shits his pants in fear. That name was indeed appropriate for me. How can a person born into an agrarian family survive if he is afraid of the dark?

We had no electricity then. I was afraid to even go to my grandmother's house, which was right behind ours, and one of my grandparents always had to escort me. I couldn't go out alone at night to pee. I couldn't sleep on a cot by myself, and so slept next to my mother, hugging her, with my legs wrapped around her. If Amma wasn't around, then I slept next to either of my grandparents. Appa didn't let me go anywhere near him. Until I was about fifteen or sixteen, I slept next to my mother. For a few years after that, I slept on a cot right next to hers. For someone like this, eruvukali was a suitable nickname.

My father not only gave me these names but also sneered and laughed as he called me by them. It made me furious. As I grew older, I became angrier. A conversation between us always ended in a fight. My father's teasing and my retaliatory anger became a daily affair. Peace returned only if Amma intervened. I often wondered what made my father hate me so much. Why was he not compassionate to me because of my nature? Why did he not show extra care? Why did he hate me instead? Why did he treat me with contempt and malice?

He died when I was twenty, and since then, I have examined our relationship from various angles.

Finally, I concluded that a particular incident was the sole reason for it. Once I came to the understanding that any father would only hate his son after such an incident, and that Appa's attitude to me was justified, I sympathised with him. It should never have happened.

We always slept by the entrance to the house, in the open courtyard between the kitchen and the thatched shed, except during winter and monsoon. Every house had at least as many cots as there were family members. We slept on these cots—never on the floor—outside the house. That is how I was introduced to the skies.

The sky's seasonal and everyday changes became etched in my heart. Even today, I can identify Aara Meen, Seven Sisters, and Uzhukkol Meen, Orion's Belt. I grew familiar with the daily changes in the moon. The shape of the waxing moon, the time of its rise and the duration of its movement across the sky, I grew to know all this. Similarly, I also learnt the patterns of the waning moon. It is important for a farmer to know about night and day, and this came to me naturally. Equally, I was enthralled by the experience of sleeping in the open, with the winds.

The cot on which Amma and I slept was in the middle of the courtyard, flanked by my father's and brother's cots on either side. I was afraid of sleeping in one of the cots in the corner, so I always slept in between. Once asleep, I did not wake up until the morning. If I did, I remembered nothing of what transpired.

Sometimes there was a strong breeze or it rained, and on winter mornings, it turned cold. On these occasions, we woke up and moved our cots into the kitchen. Often, I didn't remember waking up or moving inside. Upon waking, I would be confused about why I was sleeping in the kitchen. But that's all right.

There have been times when, woken up from my sleep, I have screamed in delirium and run around in the dark. But I was never conscious when this happened. During such episodes, I have been carried to a priest in the middle of the night because it looked like I had been possessed by evil spirits. I usually regained my senses once the priest applied vibhuti on my forehead and sprinkled holy water on my face. I became normal and clear-headed on the way back, but would have no memory of what had happened before.

No matter how many times I was taken to the priest, I continued to react in the same way if woken up at night. So my family decided not to wake me. If we had to move inside, two of them would carry me as I slept on the cot, without disturbing me. I would be hugely embarrassed the next morning when my brother teased me saying, 'We carried you like a corpse.'

The incident happened when we were sleeping outside one lovely moonlit night. I must have been four or five years old and was perhaps not yet in school. I had gone to sleep after a long day of frolicking. Though I never wake up once I am asleep, that night I did. Without opening my eyes, I reached out with my hands and legs to hug Amma. My limbs cut through empty space and landed on the cot. I groped around in panic at not finding my mother, and cried out for her as I stared at the moon. Still screaming in fear, I turned to the cot nearby.

With both its hands, a shadow picked up another shadow lying atop it and threw it into the air. The shadow that landed with a thud did not rise. It lay still.

The shadow on the cot took the form of my mother and said: 'I am right here, kannu, don't be afraid,' and reached out to me. 'Nothing happened, kannu, I haven't gone anywhere. I am right here,' she said, stroking my chest, putting me back to sleep.

Much later in life, I decided that my father's animosity towards me might have stemmed from this incident. Once I reached this conclusion, all my anger against my father evaporated. Instead, I was greatly angry with myself.

6

# My Friend Manian

Amma remembered only one of my friends until the end.

Many boys of my age visited our home when I was young. This lot included those who worked in the shop we owned in the cinema theatre. It was hard to recall someone specific from among them. In a theatre, people come and go—a person who is around one day may not be at hand the next. My friends too visited my house right from when I was in school. They tended to come separately, and then my mother wouldn't see them again for a few months or even years. When I started teaching in a college, an endless stream of students too visited me. Amma did recognise those who came frequently, but she didn't know them beyond their names. There was a reason why she distinctly remembered this friend of mine.

My parents had occasional fights. Almost always, it was about my father's drinking habits. By and large, these were verbal quarrels, but sometimes they veered out of control and Appa would end up hitting Amma. When I was ten or eleven, I began reacting fiercely when he beat her. I used to be blinded by anger back then. I hit him with any object I could lay my hands on, like firewood, or I hurled stones and utensils at him. I behaved like a madman. Fearing the backlash, Appa spoke less when I was around. Amma too raised her voice when they fought, and I detested that too. I would order her to keep quiet. If she didn't listen, I got angry with her as well. So they wound up their fights quickly if I was around.

One morning during the summer vacation after my class ten exams, my father came home drunk on toddy. My brother had left to mind our shop and I was in the goat pen. What started as an ordinary conversation between my parents soon escalated, and Appa slapped Amma so hard across her cheek that the earring she was wearing broke and a white stone fell off. Seeing me return, my father left home, afraid that I would turn wild with anger. As I reached home, I heard the sound of his Suvega moped leaving. I saw my mother's red cheeks and her tears and was furious. I rushed out to catch him, but Amma stopped me.

'Is this new for me? Neither his drinking or beatings can be stopped. Either he should die, or I should. This won't end till then,' she said, weeping. I was restless throughout the day. A home plagued by petty quarrels is hell.

I was beginning to develop a deep interest in reading books and writing poetry around this time, and I felt that the situation at home was hindering my creativity.

After some time, Amma stopped crying and resumed her work. I felt fatigued and my mind wandered. I thought of ways to leave that hell. By the afternoon, my desire to leave had become strong. I had no idea where I would go. But a voice deep within prodded me and it sounded inviting. I decided to respect it and waited for the right time.

Later that afternoon, Amma milked the cows and left to supply to the housing board colony nearby. Having failed in her desperate attempts to cover up her puffed cheeks, tear-stained face and broken earring, she left in silence. This was the opportunity I had been waiting for.

'Do not look for me,' I wrote on a small piece of paper. Then, I deflated the back tyre of my cycle.

My grandmother was sitting on the porch. We had to inform her whenever we left home, it was just something we did. I told her that, since my cycle was punctured, I was taking a bus to our shop. In the khakhi bag I took to school, I packed some clothes. That was about it. Never having left town on my own before, I had no idea what I was doing. I did not know where I was going or what I was going to do—only that I had to leave.

When I reached the bus stop, a bus to Salem arrived. I boarded and bought a ticket. Only as the bus moved did I realise where I could go. I decided to go to Chennai, get into the movies, write lyrics for songs and become famous. It was a pleasant thought. I fantasised about my success, as if people in Chennai were only waiting for me. I was barely fourteen, but having read several books by Kannadasan, I dreamed about making it big in the cinemas. And I was naïve enough to believe that my infantile jottings were poetry.

Something else struck me in the bus—my batchmate from class nine, Manian, lived in Salem. I wondered if I should visit his place and take him along to Chennai. He too was interested in films. He wanted to do scriptwriting, screenplay, dialogue and direction. He had even promised that I would be the lyricist for his debut movie.

Manian came to our village for a year to study. His was a large family of two elder sisters, a younger sister, an elder brother and a younger brother. They had converted to Christianity, so he was also called Francis Xavier. On seeing his family's difficulties, a pastor from our village had brought Manian along so he could pursue his education. That is how we came to study together for a year, and we became very close.

He knew a lot more about cinema than I did, and could reel off endless trivia. With his carefree attitude, he was a joy to be around. We spent our school intervals bantering and laughing. Even when the other boys played, we would sit in a corner chatting away. He was a natural storyteller. Being around him lessened all my worries.

At the end of the academic year, Manian discontinued his schooling and returned to Salem. Another friend and the two of us took a photograph together. Manian and I wrote to each other regularly and he visited us a couple of times. Because I wrote to him almost every week, I knew his address. When I reached Salem, I managed to find my way there. It would be good if his troubles too vanished along with mine, I thought.

His entire family lived in a two-room house and ran a shop in Sevapettai that sold cotton seeds and other fodder for cattle. He was smart, and on seeing my face and the bag, he knew right away that I had run away from home. I stayed the night at his house, and we spent all night chatting and roaming the streets of Salem. It turned out that he knew more about both cinema and life than I. He convinced me that the best thing for me was to return home and continue studying. Manian was a champion talker, wasn't he? I hold him responsible for my non-starter cinema career.

The next morning, I had breakfast with him and boarded a bus back home. I was clear-headed and determined to complete my education, no matter what, certain that only graduating from school could liberate me from my home. Manian's words still rang in my ears. 'I was not lucky enough to study. You must. After you finish your education and develop more skills, we will go to Chennai. You are the lyricist in my debut film. There's no change in that,' he had said.

By this time, there was a huge commotion at home because I had gone missing. On rummaging through my things, my parents discovered Manian's letters and his address. Along with a few relatives, they boarded a bus to Salem. They were on their way there as I was heading back. It would have been good for us to have spotted each other when our buses crossed. But life does not create such opportunities. They reached Salem and enquired about me at Manian's. When they heard that I had boarded a bus back home, they returned in peace.

Amma came home and asked me, 'How could you ever think of abandoning me? Didn't I bring you up with all the love in my heart? How could you desert me like this? I was hoping that you would take care of me until I die. What will I do if you go away? If you ever leave me again, I'll leave this world forever.'

Amma was grateful to Manian for persuading her boy to return home. After that, he and I visited each other often. A relationship bloomed between the two families as well. When he needed a loan for his elder sister's marriage, I was hesitant to part with the money I had saved up for my education. When I shared this with my mother, she told me, 'We should help anyone in distress and he was the one who gave you back to us. You must do at least this for him,' and put my doubts to rest.

My friendship with Manian was a long-term one. He stayed at my place several times after that incident. Often, he made my mother laugh with stories of things that happened in his family. She thoroughly enjoyed them. He was by my side on every important family occasion. As time passed by, our lives changed drastically and we lost touch. Amma asked about him frequently. 'Where is your friend Manian? Ask him to come over some time, I'd like to see him,' she would say. I had no idea where he lived, and couldn't contact him.

When we did get back in touch, Amma was no more. She had yearned to see him; he felt bad that he hadn't seen her one last time. That I was not able to fulfil her wish will remain my lasting regret.

# 7

# The Thousand-Eyed Shirt

For some time, Amma supplied milk to an elderly gentleman who ran a clothing store. He owned a small establishment, which he continued to run even after his sons had branched out to manage their own successful businesses. He came from a community of weavers and was also a shrewd businessman.

Though his wife always paid the monthly bill for the milk, one time, the old man came to settle the dues with Amma. As he was handing over the money, he asked her, 'Where do you buy your clothes?' Amma couldn't respond immediately.

We didn't shop in any particular store. We were not rich enough to, and often bought our clothes at the market, where we found beautiful floral-print shirts. For Deepavali and Pongal, depending on how much we could afford to spend, we bought clothes from a shop chosen at random. Since we studied in a government school, my brother and I always had two pairs of khaki trousers and four white shirts, bought at the beginning of the academic year. The thick khaki fabric for the trousers came from just about any shop.

My father always wore khakhi shirts—which is what people working in soda shops wore back then—and a lungi. Since they were the first generation to wear shirts, perhaps the workers chose it as their uniform because it concealed dirt and was comfortable. My father's shirts were stitched from the same fabric as our trousers. We used the second-rate coarse white yarn available at weaving workshops for our shirts, which were so sturdy that they never wore out. It was Amma's responsibility to outfit the entire family. She knew our needs and bought clothes accordingly.

The clothing store owner had asked Amma that question knowing nothing of our shopping habits. She first stumbled, then managed to answer: 'The shops have variety, but the market is cheap.' Laughing, he replied, 'We have a variety of clothes and they are affordable too. You could come by and buy some if you like. You don't need to pay immediately either. It can be deducted monthly from our payment for the milk.' The offer of instalments got Amma thinking.

Though none of us had ever felt the need for clothes before, we suddenly developed new kinds of wants. 'Looks like we need an entire clothing store,' Amma said.

I was on vacation after completing class eleven and needed my usual two pairs of pants and four shirts for the next academic year. It had been a year since I had shifted from khaki to a smoother fabric for the trousers and my white shirts were made of polyester now. I insisted on these this year too. News of the instalment scheme proposed by the shop owner spread among milk-vending women, and a few others too wanted to come along to the store.

The shop owner told my mother, 'Bring how many ever people you like, ma. But I don't know them. You have to take responsibility for the money. Please collect it every month and hand it over to me.'

Appa was against the idea. 'Will you go stand in front of each woman's house every month and ask for money? They won't be as keen to repay it as they will be when buying clothes. You will have to shell out money yourself to repay him,' he warned. So Amma took only one really close friend of hers, Sengamma, when she went to the shop one afternoon.

It was a tiny shop, as if two petty shops had been joined together. But it had a surprising variety of clothes for men and women of all ages. The shop owner not only offered them a seat but also served them tea bought from a shop across from his. Amma had not experienced such hospitality even in her relatives' homes. After quoting the price of each fabric, he added, 'I'll reduce a rupee just for you.' Both women were very happy that he was bringing down the price especially for them.

They bought more clothes than they had planned. After she selected the fabric for my khaki pant and white shirt, Amma spotted a white cloth, designed like the eyes of a sieve. She loved it.

'Is this meant for a shirt?' she asked the owner.

'Yes, ma. It's a good design. It will look really nice when stitched and worn.' When he spread out the pure white silky fabric for her to see, Amma felt as if a thousand eyes had opened and were looking at her. She decided it would look good on me and bought it.

The owner handed them a note that laid down the monthly instalments for a term of six months. Amma gave the fabric for stitching in a tailoring shop right next door, along with old clothes of mine as measurement. Back home, she kept praising the hospitality of the shop owner and the range of clothes in that tiny shop. 'The clothes kept coming endlessly, like tamarind pulled out in bits and pieces from the pot.'

Everything was fine.

A week later, Amma brought back the stitched clothes. I too liked the sieve-eyed shirt and looked forward to wearing it to school.

I cycled six miles to school. Before leaving, I had to finish several chores, including cleaning the loom. By the time I finished all the work and got to school, the bell had rung. My shirt was drenched in sweat and stuck to my back. I parked my cycle and joined the morning assembly line. All my friends were in white shirts as usual. The eyes in my shirt looked at them with contempt. The boys too kept staring at me.

When we were singing *Tamil Thai Vazhthu*, some of my friends were struggling to control their laughter. It seemed they were laughing at me.

The route to school was flanked by tamarind trees. Sometimes, the birds on these trees, seeing people hurrying below, shat on them. Wondering if perhaps bird droppings had fallen on me, I slowly examined my shirt. I could see nothing. Could it have fallen on my back? As the assembly progressed with the pledge, announcements and *Thirukkural* recitation, my friends' laughter grew and spread to others. As soon as the national anthem was over, the entire class thronged me.

One of them caught hold of my shirt and pinched me. Others followed. Was I getting pinched for the new shirt? Unable to bear the pain, I screamed, 'Leave me alone!' and ran towards the classroom. They chased me and kept pinching me. When the boy who sits next to me pinched my chest, I asked him what this was about. With an odd look on his face and still laughing, he said, 'If you're a girl, this is how you'll get pinched.' Then, he explained, 'If you wear a shirt made of fabric meant for a blouse, aren't you a girl?'

I tried hard not to let my angst show. The teacher too looked shocked and asked me, 'What is this, da?'

When I was a child, because there were no boys of my age in the family, I used to play with my uncle's daughters. We usually played games meant for girls, like five stones and pallankuzhi. Since I was an expert in these, my relatives called me 'pombalasatti'. Though I didn't understand what it meant then, I knew it was derogatory. I was enraged every time someone called me that. People used it to taunt me. Not knowing better, I would get mad and create a scene. It took me a long time to realise that they actually enjoyed my tantrums. Since I already had such a nickname, I felt deeply humiliated by this shirt incident.

I was now sixteen, and was becoming aware of my masculinity. Hanging my head in shame, with tearful eyes, I tried to swallow the humiliation. But it didn't work. All eyes were still on me. Several sets of sharp nails came together to pinch me. I was besieged by jeering smiles. 'Pombalasatti' filled my ears. Even teachers in the following classes treated me like an exhibit.

My classmates surrounded me during the small intervals between classes. They had all kinds of questions. I did not venture outside the classroom even during the toilet break. How would I explain why I had chosen this fabric for my shirt? I had never been so angry with Amma as I was on that day. It was Amma who comforted me whenever I was called a pombalasatti. But today, I was an object of ridicule because of her.

During the lunch break, I quickly hopped on to my cycle and rode away. I had never cycled as fast, not looking this way or that. As soon as I reached home, I dropped the cycle and my bag, took off my shirt in a frenzy and flung it at my mother. She was eating her meal under the shade of a tree in front of our house. She rushed to me in a panic, asking, 'What happened? What happened, kannu?' and held me. Everyone knew of my uncontrollable temper.

When Amma heard what had happened, she abused the shop owner: 'That dog said I could stich a shirt out of that fabric! I was naïve to believe him. How could that old man have done such a thing just to get rid of an unsold piece of cloth?'

That evening, Amma went to the shop owner's house and threw the shirt on his floor. She also settled the money she owed him, after balancing their milk bill. 'Would you eat shit for the sake of money? Even the seller in the market would have told me about the fabric. I had no clue. But could the shopkeeper be clueless? Shouldn't you have said something? A grown boy came home crying. I am done with you,' she screamed at him. She refused to listen to their explanations and also stopped supplying milk to them.

I didn't go to school that entire week; I had never taken leave from school before. Amma tried her best to console me and help me overcome my humiliation. When I finally got ready to go to school, Amma asked, 'My boy, shall I accompany you to school?'

# 8

# The Iron Handcuffs

Four or five decades ago, medical facilities were nothing like they are today. Nor did we go to a hospital as soon as someone fell ill. Occult medical practices were popular in the villages, and the primary cause of illness was possession by spirits. Since there was no electricity, ghosts were free to roam around in the dark. Dried palm fronds appeared like ghosts sitting down to take a shit. Small animals looked like apparitions before they disappeared into the darkness.

Ghosts entered the heads of those who caught a glimpse of these visions and terrified them. Some ghosts caused fever, others caused convulsions. There were ghosts who paralysed memories and caused delirium. Health issues were a competition between the ghost and the human mind.

Certain paths were best avoided even in the afternoons if you were walking alone. Tamarind trees were the ideal residence for ghosts, who could cause a whirlwind of dry leaves to rise sky-high.

God was of course the first medicine for any illness caused by spirits. Since gods could not manifest in person, they had allotted the task of warding off spirits to the temple priests.

Depending on the kind of illness, the priest would consecrate some vibhuthi with chants. He would pinch the sacred ash between the tips of his thumb and forefinger and fling it on the affected person's head like a small stone. This stone has fallen on my head many times. Sacred water would be splashed without warning, like a slap on the face, to drive away fear of the ghost. Some priests banished spirits by thrashing the person with neem leaves.

Many priests did not stop with sacred ash, but also recommended antidotes, vows and offerings to a chosen deity. Often, this included offering pongal or sacrificing animals. Other suggestions included presenting mud figurines to the deity and planting a spear at Ayyanar temples. Some deities specifically demanded the sacrifice of hens and roosters. Others asked for the offering of a ram. Depending on the severity of the illness, the priest intuited whether a hen or a ram was to be offered.

Our home always had roosters and rams that were promised to a deity. But the list of sacrificial offerings only kept growing. We have even gone to the Allah temple in town to ward off evil spirits. At any given time, there were always a couple of amulets on the traditional thread around my hips. Whenever I returned home from the town I was studying in, Amma's eyes would automatically fall on my hips to check if I was wearing the amulets. If they were missing, a new one would be brought home the very next day. A new amulet had to be worn on the hand for the first three days, only then could it be transferred to the hips. Amma wore an amulet on her upper arm until the day she died.

We would go to a hospital only when the illness could not be contained by these practices. There were only two instances when Amma acknowledged the importance of modern medicine. One was Amma's first pregnancy. It was a lasting regret for her that she could have saved her first child if she had visited a hospital sooner.

The second instance was when my elder brother, then six years old, had fever. He did not respond to any prayers, vows or entreaties to god. The fever was so high one night that he had convulsions. Amma's first son had died in her womb, and she was now worried that she might lose a second one after having raised him for six years.

It was the middle of the night. Appa was passed out drunk and would not awaken. Whom could she turn to at that hour? She wrapped a wet cloth around her son's forehead and hoisted him on to her shoulders. He looked like a piece of mere rag. She walked four miles in the middle of the night to her elder sister's house in the city.

Periyamma was shocked to see my brother's condition. They went to a doctor who lived nearby and woke him up. The doctor treated my brother at that unearthly hour and gave him a painful 'narambusi'—penicillin was often referred to as a 'nerve injection'. The fever subsided in a while. Amma praised forever the doctor who had saved her son. Nevertheless, this did not dent her belief in occult medicine.

Amma was well acquainted with all the temple priests in our region. They played a major role in the stories of our upbringing. She had an inexhaustible list of the illnesses that had struck us, how old we had been when it happened, the temple priest who had cured it, whether he had done it with ash or with neem leaves, the vows for various deities, those that were fulfilled and those that were yet to be fulfilled. We had many pending vows made to our family deity Kariyakaliamman. When we could no longer keep track of our debts to her, Kariyakali herself showed us the way.

Once, when Amma went to make an offering of newly pressed castor oil at the temple, she asked the priest, 'I owe her so much that I cannot clear my debts in this birth.

What can I do?' Well versed with what to do under such circumstances, the temple priest suggested a remedy: 'Let's cast flowers and ask Aaya for an answer. Ask her if you can accumulate all your debts on one ram and offer it to her. Tell her she ought to know your plight. If she gives us permission, we can clear all your debts to her.'

Amma cast flowers before the god and picked one at random to know the god's will. 'Kariyakaliamma, who else do I have other than you? You know the situation you have put me in. I don't have the strength to clear all the debts I owe you. Please take it all together. I offer it to you as one ram. Give us your consent, Aaya,' Amma prayed with all her heart.

Kariyakali was the goddess of our hearts and took our side, no matter what. She gave us her consent with the very first flower that Amma picked. Since it would take several years to rear a ram at home and offer it, we bought a sturdy one at the market and cleared our debts.

But the prayers and promises of offerings continued. A few incidents further strengthened Amma's belief in occult medicine. I was involved in an important one.

A month before my second-semester exams in my first year of college, I fell ill. It was an odd illness—I grew to detest the very sight of food. Even if I did manage to eat a little, I could not keep it down. I would instantly develop a severe headache and my temples would throb. The headache would get worse and I would throw up. Only after all the food I ingested came out would the headache gradually subside. I could avoid food, of course. But then, how would I live?

I was thin to begin with, and now I looked like a skeleton. None of the temple priests from near or far could cure me. English medicine too let me down. We went to Erode where several big hospitals were coming up. Plenty of medicines and tablets were prescribed, but I could not keep any of them down. The vomiting was so severe that it felt like my intestines would come out.

I got my eyes tested and wore spectacles for the headache. But I was unable to wear the glasses even for a moment. An inner voice kept urging me, 'Throw it away! Throw it away!' Enslaved to that voice, I would throw my glasses away. I held on to dear life, sustained by the sips of water I managed to have. With a swollen head and a body like a stick, I looked like something barely human lying on the cot.

I felt that only death could redeem me. I wanted to die. But when I saw Amma desperate to somehow save the son she had raised with all her love, I wanted to live too. At a stage when all hope was lost, she heard of a person who practised occult medicine rather far away. To reach him, Amma led me—seventeen years old then—holding my hand and sometimes supporting me against her shoulder, in and out of buses. We had to walk half a mile from the road. She almost carried me all the way.

The person we went to see was not a full-time temple priest but a palm-tree climber. He lived with his wife and three children in a small thatched shed in an isolated place filled with numerous palms, like many other palm-tree climbers. He asked us to wait at the Karuppanarsamy temple nearby and left to climb a tree.

Strings of iron handcuffs hung from the spears impaled on the temple ground. The cuffs were the kind that could lock both wrists together. They adorned the rusty spears like garlands. The cuffs hanging beneath the spears looked new. The atmosphere was frightening. I lay down all curled up, with my head on Amma's lap.

The priest finished tapping toddy—we still had toddy shops back then—and came back to the temple when the sun was high in the sky. He was moderately tall and his body was as dark as the palm tree. He did not look like a priest in the slightest.

After showering, he came over with a wet towel around his waist and his body still moist, and prostrated before the deity. He sat there, with mud plastered all over him and emptied out the small basket in front of him. Beautiful round pebbles tumbled out. As he enquired about us, the priest picked up a handful of them. He joined his palms, prayed to the god, opened his palms again and threw the pebbles on the ground. Then he began to separate the pebbles in twos to determine whether the last was a pair or a single one. He did this a couple of more times. We called this method 'kodu parthal', usually done with stones, castor seeds or tamarind seeds by separating them into ones and twos to know the will of god. The divination revealed that I was affected by an evil spirit. The priest told us that I would be cured if we performed a poosai for Karuppanarsamy and wore the handcuffs on my wrists.

He held out a paper with a long list and said that the poosai could be done whenever we bought all the materials. He also told us where to buy the iron handcuffs for the deity. Keeping in mind my condition and not wanting to drag me back another day, Amma decided to leave me behind and fetch all the necessary things from the town so that the poosai could be done that very day. The priest too agreed. Amma was only troubled at the thought of leaving me behind, but the priest promised to look after me.

On her way out, she kept turning back to look at me, and my eyes welled up on seeing this. It was clear that she did not want to leave me behind, but did she have a choice? I kept looking at Amma till she dissolved into a tiny dot. By then, the priest had gone out into the fields and come back with a small pot of fermented toddy. After placing it before the deity and getting his blessings, he poured some in a small cup and handed it to me. Though I was keen to have toddy, afraid of the retching that would follow, I refused.

'This has been offered to the deity. Karuppanar himself is going to enter your stomach. Nothing will happen. If you do feel like vomiting, throw up on his face. What sort of a god is he if he can't help the ones who place their faith on him?' he asked, agitated.

I gulped mouthfuls of the Karuppanar toddy, and my stomach felt cool. It felt full and even slightly bloated, something I hadn't experienced in a long time. But I continued to be nervous, expecting my head to throb any minute and the toddy to come out as vomit. The priest stroked my chest and smeared a handful of the black ash strewn before Karuppanar on my stomach. It was indeed a miracle, nothing happened to me. The toddy stayed in my stomach. I let out a burp and my stomach felt lighter. It had been days since I had felt such lightness.

I was mildly intoxicated already and about to fall asleep on the mud floor when the priest brought another cupful of toddy and made me sip from it, resting my body against his. I don't know how much of it I drank. My thin body grew more intoxicated. I fell asleep—a deep, quiet sleep after a long time.

I woke up to voices. The sun had gone down and it was late evening. Amma had placed a big basket filled with poosai items before Karuppanar. A rooster with its legs tied up lay against the basket. It was the red rooster from our house.

When his frightened eyes fell on me, he made a feeble sound, flapped his feathers and tried to crawl towards me.

The priest was getting ready to climb again. He had a coir rope around his waist, a box attached to his back and a climbing rope on his shoulder. 'Stay put. I will come back after work. If you have brought something for your son, give him a little. Don't worry. Will it refuse to stay in his stomach in front of Karuppanar? He can be worshipped only at night. My family members will come. Don't be afraid.' Then he walked away towards the palm trees.

Amma fed me a few mouthfuls of the rasam rice she had brought with her. I was confident that Karuppanar, who had helped me keep the toddy in my stomach, would do the same with the rice too. The energy that shone on my face after I had woken up must have inspired confidence in Amma. Both of us kept looking at my stomach, now bloated with rasam rice. My temples did not make their presence felt. We were both happy that I would survive. Amma ate the leftover rasam rice. It was probably her first meal of the day.

After nightfall, the priest's wife, son and two daughters came to the temple with a lantern. His wife lit earthen lamps, while the young kids ran around the fields and played. I sat leaning against the spear. His wife continued to make arrangements for the poosai as she chatted with my mother.

Karuppanar, who was a small stone set in the mud, now dazzled with sandal paste and kungumam. The silver eyes that Amma had bought were now on Karuppanar and it looked as if he was staring at me. Placed before him were flowers, fruits, some rice on a tray, packets of grains and other poosai items. The iron handcuffs my mother had bought were smeared with ash and also placed before the god. Lemons were lying in a huge heap. The priest came after a long time, wearing a wet cloth around his waist, as he was in the morning, and carrying a small pot of toddy for Karuppanar.

The priest made me sit before the god. His wife and my mother went towards the children playing in the field. It was just the three of us—the priest, Karuppanar and I. Taking off my clothes, I tied the white cloth that the priest gave me around my waist.

Chanting illegibly, the priest started the poosai. His voice began feebly and then rose fiercely and then fell again. I was not scared. What was there to fear when one had been this close to death? He poured some of the fermented toddy placed before Karuppanar into his hands and sprinkled it on my head. When I was not expecting it, he splashed some hard across my face. He also gave me some to drink. Then he asked me to stand up and stroked me from head to toe thrice with the iron handcuffs. Fastening them on my hands, he asked me to sit down.

I was shirtless and shivered in the cold. He gave me some more toddy to drink. As soon as the toddy entered my body, the shivering decreased. Each time he asked me to pray with folded hands, I did so. Towards the end, something wild got hold of him and he bit the rooster's neck as it wailed, and spat the blood on Karuppanar. The rooster writhed in agony and bled to death. He asked me to remove the handcuffs and place it before the god. As I did that, I cried. I wailed and gasped by turns, and then fell down.

The temple was my refuge that night and I slept well. Amma would not have slept at all. The next morning, we worshipped Karuppanar again and were ready to leave.

'For one month, give the boy toddy of a single tree. He will recover,' the priest said.

And that was how I got better. I regained my appetite gradually and in a month, recovered fully.

In later years, I began to lose faith in god and questioned and mocked everything. Amma would remind me of the iron handcuffs and say, 'You would have died then if not for Karuppanar. Would you have been able to talk like this?'

That would shut me up. What could I have possibly said?

# 9

# The Book Addict

For Amma, paper was just an item of utility. The provisions she bought in the market were wrapped in paper. Cumin seeds, pepper and mustard seeds were packaged in small pieces of paper and tied with a thread, while grains, pulse varieties and roasted bengal gram were packed in large paper bags. Though we did not have to buy grains and pulses because we grew them in our fields, our supply of roasted bengal gram and spices came from the market. After emptying the provisions into their boxes, Amma would carefully save the pieces of paper and the paper bags in a basket. If she found loose papers lying around anywhere, she picked those up as well and brought them home. Amma was really fond of paper.

This was because papers were particularly useful to light the stove with. People who use firewood will appreciate this. Dead palm fronds and dry leaves were just as good, but they were not as easy to store as paper, which could be stuffed into a basket. Nothing worked like paper when it rained—one only had to stack up the firewood with sufficient space for air to pass through, place a piece of paper beneath it and light it up. The wood would catch fire immediately.

My brother and I were instructed to keep papers torn from our school notebooks in this basket. Amma would rage wild and scold if she caught us throwing any loose papers away. If there was none around to light the stove with, Amma tore a few pages from the back of our notebooks, which was a bit of a problem. If the sheet of paper torn off was attached to another in which we had taken notes, that too would come off. We would then pick a fight with Amma, at the end of which we usually declared that we were going to bunk school. 'The teachers will beat me up. I can't go to school!' We never missed an opportunity to miss school. Amma would struggle to placate us and send us off.

At the end of every academic year, we sold our school books to the incoming batch of students at half their original price. Students were eager to buy books that had the binding and pages intact. We could also score a few vadais from a tea stall if we gave the pages from our used notebooks after removing the hard binding. Amma didn't want us to do this, though. She would tie the notebooks with a thread and stack them away. That would be enough kindling for at least a couple of months. Enough stock to tide over the monsoon, Amma would say. Those were the days when it did rain during the rainy season.

But there also came a time when Amma began to despise paper. When I was in class eight, Anna and I started buying magazines like *Rani*, *Ananda Vikadan* and *Kumudam*. Amma thought this was an unnecessary expenditure. Once we got hold of these magazines, Anna and I couldn't do anything else until we finished reading them. Sometimes we bought a copy each. Amma hated it; besides the money being wasted, work was also getting affected. These magazines also occasionally carried glamorous pictures of actresses. 'Are you spending money to buy and read these kind of books?' Amma would ask furiously. Soon, she gave up the habit of collecting paper because she could now tear pages from our magazines when she needed to.

Presently, she had to face another issue. When I was in class nine, I started buying literary books. None of the shops in our village sold them, so I ordered them through VPP after seeing advertisements in magazines. The postman would deliver the books and collect the money. Amma would silently watch me hand the money over. The loathing and anger on her face could scorch.

As soon as the postman left, she would begin ranting, going on and on, and there was no way I could read the book then.

I would go and sit somewhere in a field and not return for a long time. Though Amma would call out loudly enough, I would pretend not to hear and return home only after dark.

'He forgets everything around him when he has a book in his hand. At this rate, is he going to have the time to study well, become a district collector and give all his money to me? I graze goats and cows, sell milk diluted with water and save every paisa. This dog throws all our money at paper! I don't know how he is going to survive!' and so on and on she grumbled.

I used to buy a book every month. Amma's tirade would begin the day the book arrived, and by the time it subsided, the next one would come. Her cycle of rants would start up again. To avoid this, I told the postman not to deliver the books to our home and picked them up from the post office instead. However, Amma would find me reading the book, and know what I had done. She remembered the covers of all my books and recognised a new one instantly.

Though I also had a membership in the public library, it did not have the books I needed, nor did it stock any new ones. It was tiring to search for books there. I was deeply interested in poetry around this time. There was an unwritten rule that the public library could not purchase contemporary poetry. Traditional poetry ran for many pages, but the contemporary books had a lot of blank space, with three or four lines printed in a corner on just one side of a page. Why would one buy books with so many empty pages? This is what the then education minister, and others in positions of responsibility and authority, must have thought. Perhaps a professor who detested contemporary poetry was a member of the committee that selected books for the library. I, who had a deep interest in poetry, did not find sufficient fodder in the public library. I was forced to buy books.

Predictably, Amma had a problem with allotting space in the house for my books. But I negotiated and secured a stool to stack them on. She reproached me every time she laid eyes on that stool. Then I managed to find a wooden box for my books. She complained that it took up too much space in the house. I was afraid that she would sell my books by the kilo to a scrap store when I was away. The one thing Amma disliked about me was my habit of buying books and we frequently quarrelled over it. 'Mad fellow! Mad fellow!' she often said.

The more Amma scolded me, the deeper grew my fascination with books. I threatened her every day when leaving home: 'Don't you dare misplace my books on the pretext of cleaning or sweeping the house. If you do, I'll never come back.'

My obsession with books was a huge source of trouble. It was my bane to constantly roam around in search of them.

I named my brother's daughter, born in 1985, Elamathi. Nonetheless, to check if there were better names, I ordered a book titled *Names for Babies* from Manimekalai Publishers. Was it necessary to spend money and buy a book just for naming a child, Amma scolded me severely.

Our financial circumstances were bad those days. We hardly had any income because the cinema theatre in which my father had a shop had shut down. Appa was in poor health and was confined to the house. The meagre income from selling the milk of two buffaloes is what sustained our family. Given these circumstances, Amma could not make sense of the idea of buying a book only to name a child. Her remonstration began with 'Don't dance around without understanding the value of money,' and only grew from there.

I too provoked Amma by claiming more space for my books, from the stool to the wooden box to a wooden cupboard. When I went on to do my higher studies, Amma's rants scaled down to mutterings. Whenever I visited home, my bag was full of books. She would stare at the bulging bag and fall silent. 'Do you have money for food?' she would mock me.

From this time on, she never directly disapproved of my book-buying, but indirectly, she did express her displeasure. However, this did not trouble me and I just laughed it away. I had come to be known as 'the boy who reads' in the village. Amma allowed herself to feel a little proud of this, and perhaps that is why she now tolerated my books.

I lived and studied in Chennai for a few years, and had also got married around that time. I had by then become the owner of a substantial collection of books—many bought in Chennai, piles of them I had picked up from scrap stores, some stolen from others and so on. In 1996, I got a government job and shifted to our village with my new family. I was a college professor and the first government employee in our village—a matter of pride for Amma.

We had very few things to transport from Chennai. The ten cartons of books that we had dispatched soon reached us. Now, there were a few thousand books at home, including those that were already here.

We lived in a one-bedroom house. Where was the place for books? I built long concrete shelves on the walls to properly store them all. Amma raised no objections. She once said: 'Your father was obsessed with alcohol and beedis. Addicted to them, he tortured us until he passed away. Your elder brother is also addicted to drinking and smoking beedis. He also causes much trouble. Every human being has some addiction. Is there a person without one? You too have an addiction—books. Other than the fact that it is an expensive obsession, it doesn't trouble anyone. Go on, do as you please, buy more and stack them up to your heart's content!'

# 10

# The Corral

Our farmland was rain-fed, and cattle were important in the scheme of things. They were helpful in activities like irrigation, ploughing and husking. The cow dung served as manure. We earned more selling milk than we did from farming. The droppings of goats fertilised the land and their meat sold for a good price.

For us, agriculture revolved around the cattle. We sowed maize but harvested the corn cobs before the plants matured. Otherwise, the stems would dry up and become unsuitable for fodder and could injure the mouths of our cows. Throughout the year, cattle fodder was the most important concern for us. Similarly, we could make do if there were no rains or no yields from our groundnut plantations. What we worried about was that the creeper—round-the-year fodder for the goats—was healthy. The important tasks of harvesting the crop and drying and stacking hay were also difficult.

There were always some cows and goats in our household and the whole day's work was centred around them. The sheep grazed all day, and one of us was always watching over them. It was not easy; we had to be on our guard day and night—monitoring the pregnant ones, safeguarding the kids and managing the rams when they caused trouble. If the sheep were hungry at night, they would bleat pitiably, non-stop, and disturb our sleep. We had to shepherd them to the grazing lands and have them drink plenty of water. If they didn't manage to graze enough, we fed them dried groundnut plants and leaves of the castor plant until their stomachs were full.

It was impossible for people who had goats and cows to travel out of town for a few days. If we absolutely had to go, we would have to make arrangements for someone to look after them. We would then worry whether that person would look after them as well as we do, and that would stress us out.

Amma was closer to our goats and cattle than to most people. She named each goat and every cow, and called them by their names. She could tell apart the voices of all the goats. If one of them bleated, Amma would talk to it and it responded to her voice. At least one goat kid could be seen trailing her all the time. The goats birthed several young ones in a litter and would not have enough milk for all of them. So we would bottle-feed a couple of the kids and they would grow very fond of us. When the cow's yield was plentiful, Amma would go to the market and buy a kid, which would only be bottle-fed. These kids always followed us around and Amma loved it. She could not live without goats.

Towards the end of her life, Amma was sad that she hadn't raised goats for a few years. For an old person living alone, a single goat is all the company they need. They can share their life stories and memories with it. No human has either the time or patience to listen to old people. But all a goat needs is to be stroked—it will respond to the love and listen tirelessly.

If Amma began a conversation with: 'Let me tell you the story of my father. Listen!' or 'Let me tell you the story of my husband,' or 'Will you listen to my children's story?' the goats nodded their heads and listened. They always had a sad look plastered on their face. When Amma narrated her story, they seemed to look sad for her sake. They also occasionally bleated in empathy. 'If I just had a kid goat, my needs would be taken care of!' she often said—the income from a single goat was sufficient to put food on her plate.

I wrote many poems in my younger days. They were filled with empty dreams and fantasies because those were the kind of poems that I got to read. Taking inspiration from them and imitating them, I wrote prolifically. I participated in poetry competitions in school and college. Mistaking ornate language for poetry, I used to regard even snatches of comedy and propaganda speech as beautiful verse.

An incident from when I was a first-year undergraduate student changed my perspective. It involved Amma and the goats.

It was summer. Our house near the fields consisted of three sheds with thatched roofs—two had walls and the third only had a thatched wall. My grandparents lived in one. Since they were old and there was no electricity, they would have their dinner early and lay down on their cots. Another hut was used for cooking and to store utensils. During winter, Amma and I slept there. My father and brother used to get back home only at two in the morning after minding our shop in the cinema theatre. The shed without walls was used to store fodder for the goats and cattle and to tie up the calves. We sometimes also slept there too. On that day, Amma and I were sleeping in the cowshed.

I was fast asleep when Amma shook me awake with, 'Boy, boy!'

'What, Amma?' I asked her wearily, turning over in the cot, trying to hold on to my sleep.

'Get up and come out, da!'

I understood that it was something important and immediately jumped up. Outside, the breeze was cooler than it should have been in summer. The wind raised dust that swirled about noisily. I still wanted to get back to bed.

'Why did you wake me up, Amma?' I asked angrily.

'See how the wind is rushing! Did you see the sky above? The clouds are gathering. There will be both wind and rain. If you sleep with the thatches open, the wind will carry everything away. Then, we'd have to beat our stomachs and chest and cry over losing this and that.'

I realised the gravity of the situation. Summer showers never came alone and were always accompanied by fierce winds and heavy rains. We usually secured the sheds with ropes to protect them from the winds—we pulled these and tied them even tighter. We collected all our things and brought them in. We tied the buffalo calf inside the thatched shed.

The wind was blowing dust into our faces and we could not even lift our heads up to see. I had a torchlight in my hand. Stacks of groundnut and maize hay were stored in the field a little distance away. They were tied to a rock with ropes attached to four big stones we had placed around them. We checked if they were all right. Unable to bear the force of the wind, a drumstick tree nearby fell. Amma construed it as an omen. The leaves of the palm tree swayed in the wind like a demon.

'God knows what the wind and rain are going to take away today!' Amma said.

The sheep were bleating fearfully in unison; we could hear them. We ran towards our corral in the field. The tarpaulin tied with ropes was threatening to shake loose. We checked the knots and then, pushing aside the tarpaulin, we went in. The sheep were huddled together in the middle of the corral, with their heads stuck to each other's stomachs.

Sheep are known to have herd mentality, they always follow the one next to them. If the first sheep in a herd falls into a pit, the others will follow behind, goes a saying. We had bonded closely with the sheep and understood them well. They have the ability to sense danger and are a united lot.

The sight of them huddled together so tight, as if they were braided together, is something I will never forget. When they heard Amma, they started bleating pitiably. The shed swayed in the wind.

Amma separated three kids hiding amidst the sheep and handed them to me. I slung one across my shoulder, held the other two in my arms, lifted the tarpaulin and ran homewards. The kids were wailing and they weighed me down.

I reached home, covered them with a big basket and ran back to the corral. The rain now joined the wind. The draught swirled the rain into a whip and lashed my back. I kept my face down to avoid the gale and continued to run.

Amma stood inside, holding down the shed as the wind tried to lift it off the ground. A tug-of-war ensued between Amma and the wind. The sheep remained huddled together. I held the other side of the hut and pulled it down. Could even our combined strength match that of the gale? It lifted both of us along with the hut a clear one foot off the ground and then dropped us. The rope that held the tarpaulin broke. The corral rattled in the wind and looked as if it would rip apart any moment now.

We knew that nothing could be done.

'Untie the ropes of the tarpaulin. Let the sheep run whichever way they want. We can find them after the rains stop. We can't do anything else,' Amma said.

I untied the ropes and stepped outside the tarpaulin. Only then did Amma step out of the shed. As soon as she did, the fierce wind uprooted the hut. The timing was perfect. We were stunned to see the shed fly like a bird with giant wings and then fall to the ground against the backdrop of lightning in the sky. Once the shed was gone, the sheep ran amok in the dark.

Amma took my arm in hers. We tore through the wind and rain and somehow managed to reach home. It poured incessantly for an hour after that. We stepped out once it was over, herded the sheep and patched up the tarpaulin.

That night's experience left a deep imprint in my mind. I wrote it out as a long poem, pouring all my emotions into it. I had the satisfaction of capturing a great experience and took pleasure in reading it many times over. I realised that all my previous poems were just empty words, and considered this my true first poem. Since then, lived experiences and emotions have occupied a primary place in shaping my poetry.

It was Amma who helped me realise this truth, along with the sheep of course.

11

# 'He Is My God'

Appuchi—my maternal grandfather—was under our care for four years towards the end of his life. He had lost his wife when he was young. Though it was relatively easy for men to remarry back then, he never did. Perhaps he wanted to avoid the possibility of his two daughters being ill-treated by a stepmother. Or it might be that he valued his independence—he transported sacks of grain on a hand-drawn cart and his work took him to many different places. Whatever the reason, he never married again.

He became even more independent after his daughters got married. Whatever little land he had and the house he owned, he lost. As far back as I can remember, he had neither the hand-drawn cart nor the bulls, and instead sold onions at the market.

I went in search of him on every market day in our village. Besides giving me a full bag of onions, he always placed a rupee in my palm. A rupee was a lot of money back then. No one knew where he stayed; he had a different answer for each time that question was asked. If you wanted to see him, you had to find him at the market, and he was at a different one every day. This continued for many years.

We named him 'vaithu thatha' because of his bulging tummy; he was a burly man. Once a year, he gave us two rupees during the temple festival, sometimes even five rupees. There were rumours that he squandered his money on women and had several simultaneous relationships. Amma was always embarrassed when someone spoke of him this way. Her elder sister fought with Appuchi bitterly about the matter of women, as a result of which my grandfather was not on speaking terms with her, neither did they visit each other. He occasionally visited us.

When my brother and I were young, we used to feel left out during the school holidays. My cousins' maternal grandparents were still alive, and they spent several days with the grandparents then. They also had maternal uncles whom they visited, even during weekly holidays. There were no children in my mother's family, other than my brother and I. Whenever our cousins told us about the snacks their grandmother had made for them, the money their grandfather had given them, the gifts their uncles had given them and the games they had played with their uncles' children, we cut a sorry figure. Our grandfather's home was the market and we had no maternal uncles. Where could we go?

Amma's plight was worse than ours. She had nowhere to go to rest up. In those days, it was common for a woman to leave for her parental home after a quarrel with her husband. It was, in fact, commonly referred to as '*kobithu kondu pothal*'. The husband would go and persuade his wife to return. If either or both of them were stubborn, the wife would stay for longer at her mother's home. Eventually, the elders would intervene and strike a compromise.

My parents frequently fought. On these occasions, Amma would let her hair loose and sit in front of the house, wailing. 'If my mother were alive, I could have sought comfort in her lap! If I could visit my sister, I would have gone to her house! I have become an orphan! Even if I am beaten, kicked or killed, no one will come to my rescue or question my husband!'

My father would laugh. 'Why don't you go complain to that man with the big sagging belly? Let him come here dragging his stomach along and question me. I can handle him.'

In the month of Chitthirai, mid-April to mid-May, Appuchi came to visit, bringing us some mangoes in a bag. Fatigue was writ large on his face and body. We could actually see his exhaustion from having wandered aimlessly for so many years. When he visited us, Appuchi usually left the same evening, but that day he stayed back.

Perhaps my father read his face. When they sat on the cot in front of the house eating their dinner, Appa said, 'Mama, why do you wander like this? Stay with us. You'll be taken care of. We'll just make some extra rice, that's all.'

Amma was furious. 'Don't you have any brains? Won't people talk ill of us? How can he just sit in his daughter's house, eating for free here? This isn't necessary. Let him wander the streets as he always has. If he dies like a dog on the streets, we will perform his last rites. If he dies in some faraway place, at least four people will dispose of his body, taking him to be an orphan, won't they?' she screamed.

Appuchi remained quiet.

Appa replied, 'People will say a thousand things. How is it possible to listen to all of them? If Mama had a son, we needn't have bothered. But he doesn't have one! I am his son now. Mama, from now on, you must stay here. Stay here as you would in your own son's house. We'll take care of you.'

Amma wouldn't budge. 'It's all right for him to stay in his son-in-law's house if he had brought along a sackful of possessions. People would then say he gave away all his earnings to his son-in-law and is now eating out of that.

What does he have now? He has given everything to some woman or the other. If he comes empty-handed, how will he digest what he eats? He can visit, stay a night and then leave. He better leave when the early hours of the morning do!' she warned.

The argument between my parents came to a head.

'I could earn a lot more if my hands and legs had been strong enough. Nonetheless, I don't need to live off my father-in-law's earnings. He doesn't have to give me a single paisa! Am I running a hotel here to take money from him and then feed him? It's decided, this is where he will live now. His soul has spent many years wandering about. Let him be in one place in his last days.'

'If he stays with us, you cook for him! I will not cook an extra fistful of rice! Nor will I serve him. I will not suffer this humiliation!'

'Who are you to give him food? I will give him mine. Mama will stay here from today. Are you planning to drive away an old man? That will only embarrass me. Won't people speak ill of me, won't they say that I couldn't feed just one more person? Give him my share of food, that's enough. I'll eat if there's more or I'll go hungry!'

'Let the women he gave all his money to look after him. He's not my burden.'

'You have crossed the limits now, speaking like this about your own father! I will hit you on your mouth!'

That's when Appuchi opened his mouth. 'Mapilla, don't fight amongst yourselves. Whatever's destined for me will happen.'

'What's all this talk about destiny? I'll arrange a cot for you. You can stay here. Your daughter does not respect my words. Let's see if at least you do.'

From that day on, Appuchi lived with us.

There were soda machines inside the cowshed. The goats and calves were tied in front of the shed. We slept just outside the house in summer and inside during winter. We had another small house with a tiled roof, which we used as storage space. Every now and then, Amma slept in that house. Where would we allot space for Appuchi?

The wall behind the shed had some space for storing firewood and protecting the fodder from the rains. To access that area, we had to go around the shed. It was possible to put a cot there. We gave that space to my grandfather.

Appuchi was well fed because Amma served him on time. She would remain silent until he finished eating. He usually let out a loud burp while washing his hands, and that is when she would begin to scold him: 'Isn't it enough that you ate up all that you earned? Do you need to belch on top of that?'

If my father or someone else was around, the diatribe wouldn't stop.

'We know of parents who take in their daughter and look after her. Only here will you see a creature who sits and eats in his daughter's house without any shame!

'Doesn't he feel guilty eating without doing any work at all? Can't he move his hands and feet a bit and take care of some small task? All he does is eat, shit and sleep.

'He squandered everything someplace else. He now gets all he needs from this place. Have you ever seen such a thing?

'A man needs to understand the consequences of his actions. He needs to feel ashamed to be eating in his son-in-law's house. But this man has none of that. I have never seen someone who was a vagabond all this time, and now behaves like there's no one better than him!'

There was no restraint in Amma's abuse. No matter what she said, though, Appuchi said nothing. Silence was his language. If someone said, 'Look at your daughter, how she speaks,' in return all he said was, 'It's my daughter who talks this way. She feeds me. I'll listen to it and walk away.'

My father never said a word to hurt his father-in-law. Every time Amma spoke ill of him within his hearing, Appa would say, 'That's enough.'

Appuchi found it difficult to pass his time. He spent half the day at a tea stall in the village. His baths were long affairs. He went to the grazing fields and spent some time there. The rest of the time he was on his cot in the cowshed. He drank tea and also chewed on betel and tobacco leaves.

Appa had an account at the tea stall and asked the shopkeeper to include Appuchi's tab in it as well. Apart from this, Appa occasionally gave him a rupee or two, without Amma's knowledge. The government had introduced a pension scheme for the elderly around this time and the word on the street was that those who didn't have a son were eligible for it. It was commonly known among the people as 'money for orphans'. Appuchi applied for it. He met some people he knew in the town and somehow got the money—twenty rupees a month. The postman would take a rupee and Appuchi got nineteen, which was more than his monthly expenses.

Amma's rants too changed.

'If you don't chew this useless tobacco all day, will food refuse to go down your throat? Even a cow doesn't chew so much in a day. Your mouth always keeps chewing!

'Every morning I pour a pot of tea into your mouth, isn't that enough? Just because your tongue desires it, do you need to drink tea from the stall twice a day? If you had ever earned some money and taken care of your family, you would understand the value of money. What would someone who roamed about like a mendicant know?

'I feed you because it is my duty as your daughter. You should have bitten off your tongue and died rather than claiming money from the government by proclaiming yourself an orphan.'

There was no dearth of abuse, and soon people in the village and our relatives heard of it. 'The son-in-law is stupid. He doesn't speak a word. Only the daughter keeps ranting against her father. The old man doesn't say anything because she's his daughter. Poor man!' they said.

The words that they would have expected my father to say came instead from my mother. Whatever ill the village people could have spoken of Appuchi also came from Amma herself. She gave no one the smallest opportunity. Her abuse didn't stop, no matter what people said. If anything, it only increased by the day. It became so normal that whenever Amma ranted, Appa and Appuchi began to exchange smiles. But Amma never stopped.

After a few years, Appa had to undergo a surgery for stomach ulcer and was admitted to a hospital. Surgeries were uncommon back then and we were worried. When someone at the tea shop enquired about my father, Appuchi apparently stood up, lifting his heavy body, and bowing towards the east, said, 'He is my god. He feeds me a handful of rice at every mealtime; he is my god. He must recover quickly. If something happens to my god, I shall end my life too.'

Appuchi's proclamation, 'He is my god,' and that he had bowed spread through the village and reached Amma's ears. From that day on, she stopped hurling abuse at Appuchi.

My father's surgery was successful and he recovered well. Appuchi was alive for another year after that. As long as he lived, he worshipped my father as god.

But it was Amma who had made my father a god.

12

# THE LAST REFUGE

My parents were perfect for each other. Amma's name was Perumayi and Appa's name was Perumal. Both were born in the month of Puratasi, mid-September to mid-October, considered auspicious for its connection to Lord Tirupathi Perumal. This explains the compatibility of their names. Appa addressed Amma as 'pilla', meaning child, and in front of others he called her 'Peruma'. Amma never called my father by name. My elder brother and I were addressed as 'paiya', the colloquial term for boy, with 'older' or 'younger' appended to it to differentiate between us.

Amma also used paiya for my father. If he was at a distance, she would raise her voice and call out, 'Paiya! Paiyo!' When he was nearby, she addressed him using the single pronoun.

Our family used plural pronouns with each other as a mark of respect. If the husband and wife used the less respectful singular pronouns for each other, the children too would follow suit and address their parents the same way.

When talking to others, Amma referred to Appa as 'my son's father'. Similarly, if the eldest child in the family was a girl, then the father was referred to as 'my girl's father'.

My parents made all decisions in consultation with each other. The conversation would begin slowly and pick up pace as it progressed. They would even seem to be quarrelling, but that was how they exchanged views. Eventually, they would reach some sort of an agreement.

What did they argue about? Usually about what to sow this year, when to sell the goats and whether or not to change the thatch for the shed. Appa liked to take on challenges, while Amma was hesitant to try new things. She thought it best to conserve what we already had. But Appa would want to take that next step. At first, Amma would resist, and then give in eventually. This has always been their habit. Both of them were hard-working.

Since arrack and toddy were easily available, my father got into the habit of drinking at an early age. Though everybody in our family drank, Appa was different—he never ate after. This was okay if he had had toddy but not arrack. It is important to fill one's stomach after drinking arrack because it is heat-inducing, while toddy is a coolant. Since my father never ate after drinking, no matter what he drank, he developed stomach ulcer at an early age.

He also drank excessively and, many a day, would not even come home. Amma would go looking for him and bring him back. Otherwise, he would have either slept near the liquor shop or stumbled and passed out on his way home. If he didn't turn up before what she considered a reasonable time, Amma went looking for him. On most days, this was the norm. She would find him, bring him home, feed him and then put him to sleep. But when she served him food, he only pecked at it like a chicken. Often, he writhed in pain because of the ulcer. He didn't eat on time either. His drinking habit was Amma's biggest source of trouble.

Even the couple of mouthfuls he ate had to be something he liked. He was particularly fond of paddy rice and paruppu kuzhambu made of pigeon peas, and demanded to have lentils every day. He was happy to even have plain mashed lentils. If it was cooked with drumstick or brinjal on the side, even better. This was also what my brother wanted.

Amma made excellent curries with bitter gourd and with ladies' fingers. But if the kuzhambu had vegetables instead of lentils, or she made greens, only Amma and I would eat it. So no matter what was made, there was always some mashed lentils to be had. Appa also liked meat curries, whether chicken or mutton, and he liked the way Amma cooked them.

My parents fought most frequently about Appa's drinking habits. Amma never said anything when he was drunk, but would accost him the next day when he returned from his soda shop and was preparing to leave for a drink. Or she would speak with him after he was sober in the morning. Though she knew he would not stop drinking, Amma believed she could at least control it somewhat. She was also worried about his health. What would she do if something were to happen to him? What would the future hold for her?

When we were kids, my elder brother and I helplessly watched them fight and stood by crying. Appa wanted to avoid these rows, so he would quietly slip away without informing Amma. If she was around, he would step out on the pretext of going to take a leak behind the house. On some days, he would even drink on his way back home. He had several ways to hoodwink Amma.

Usually, their fight was only the flinging of words. Amma's tirade would simply conclude with: 'Go on, drink endlessly, scorch the family and go away!' But sometimes, things escalated. On those occasions, not wanting to prolong the argument, Appa would just slink away. Some days, Amma physically restrained him by holding on to the towel around his neck. This was usually on days when Appa's stomach ache was worse than usual, aggravating Amma's concerns. He would plead with her and cajole her. If Amma stood her ground, it would end in a quarrel. On rare occasions, he would hit her. Then Amma would flare up further and only hold on tighter. One of my paternal grandparents would have to come and separate them.

On the days she was hit, Amma would get angry and walk out. Her father was a wanderer. Her elder sister lived in a city and Amma had a love-hate relationship with her. The custom of women going to their parental homes after a fight with their husband was so common that it was also called '*seeradi kondu pothal*' because parents sometimes sent back gifts, or seer, with their daughters when their husbands took them back home.

But where did Amma have a home to bring back gifts from? She usually went to the field and lay there, hiding beneath a clump of maize plants. My father never went in search of her. My brother, my grandmother and I would go looking for her and bring her back home. 'Where could she go? She has to come back here anyway,' Appa would say confidently.

After she came home, Amma would begin her laments: 'If I had a mother, I could rest my head in her lap. If I had a father, I could complain to him and stay with him. I have no mother. My father is a good-for-nothing. I have one sibling and it's a disgrace to go to her home. What place do I have other than this five-storey palace?'

When Appa had a stomach ache, he would press and hold his midriff tightly with both hands. It was evident from his bent posture that he was truly suffering. He had to go through two operations. People were deathly afraid of surgeries back then. Amma went through some really tough times then, doing everything she could to save him at any cost.

On the one hand were financial difficulties and on the other was the issue of managing her time between the hospital and the fields. It was a difficult period for everyone in the family, including my grandparents. My grandmother stayed with Appa in the hospital, and Amma cooked and carried food for them every day. The hospitalisation lasted nearly a month.

Appa survived both surgeries. For almost a year after each surgery, he stopped drinking. Two surgeries and two years. Those were the happiest two years of Amma's life. There have been other happy periods from time to time, but these two years were the highlights.

In that time, Amma went about with a glow of contentment on her face, was extra devoted to her work and was hopeful about life. But Appa couldn't last beyond a year without his drink. He would start off saying that he wanted only a bit of toddy. It never did stop with that, though, and he fell back into his old ways.

Soon enough, he was operated on again. The doctors said that it would be difficult to save him this time. Anything that entered his stomach left it without being digested at all. His intestines developed sores and stopped functioning. Appa did not survive the surgery and died in a lot of pain. My grandmother estimated that he must have been around forty-six years old when he died. My mother would have been around forty-two then.

Amma wept inconsolably, screaming, 'My last refuge too is now gone.'

13

# White Sari

My father passed away in August 1986. I had just enrolled for my post-graduation then. According to the customs of our caste, Amma was given a white sari after Appa's death. I am not aware of how old this custom of a widow being required to wear a white sari is. I was twenty years old then—an ignorant village man with no knowledge of the outside world or any understanding of society. It never struck me that there was no need for a white sari.

In the next five years, there were several changes in the customs of our caste. Widows who were middle-aged or older were provided a saffron-coloured sari instead of a white one. The younger women were allowed 'the red sari'—as coloured saris were known—or they were referred to as 'dyed saris'. Today, not only are young widows allowed to wear a red sari but also it has become common for them to remarry. This is a huge change.

Since the white sari marked out a widow, Amma's world shrunk considerably. In the mornings, she avoided stepping out of the house. She would leave home at five to supply milk to a few houses in the housing board nearby and return before the break of dawn, when the other milk suppliers were only starting their rounds.

People were mindful of omens when setting out in the morning for a festive occasion or other important work. Amma arranged her schedule so that she could avoid running into anyone and causing them bad luck. If people ran into her, someone might even say within her earshot, 'A widow has come in front of us, let's go back.' If they dreamt about a woman clad in a white sari, they thought of her as Goddess Mariamman and rejoiced. But they didn't approve of a woman in white appearing before them in person.

Amma only attended functions she could not afford to miss, and even then, she stood inconspicuously at the back of the gathering. Though it was she who was responsible for looking after our family, when my father was alive or after he passed away, Amma had no regrets about not getting the recognition due to her. Only when faced with financial difficulties did she lament: 'Would I have to face this if that drunkard dog had been alive?' But that was all.

The most pressing problem with the white sari was its maintenance. It was tough to work in the fields or to graze buffaloes and goats while wearing it. When being milked, the buffalo would swish its tail, sending drops of dung and urine flying on to her sari. Stains really showed up on a white sari, and it was difficult to get rid of them. Detergents that proclaimed, 'Stains are good,' were not available then. Amma initially struggled with the white sari, but from her own experience and based on her discussions with others, she learnt the art of maintaining it.

Amma had three kinds of saris. For functions, the weekly market and the annual temple festival, she wore a bright white. For supplying milk or walking only a couple of miles, she used one made of power loom coarse yarn. While working at home or in the fields, she wore the cheap material of dhotis or towels and used two pieces of these—one around her waist and another to cover the upper part of her body.

Amma neither expressed any yearning for coloured saris nor any frustration over not being able to wear them. When we talked about purchasing clothes for the family, she would say, 'Am I going to wear colourful saris? Let's just buy some white sari and not a very expensive one. How different can one white sari possibly be from another, and I only ever wear it on rare occasions.' Though she would say this with a smile, I wasn't able to bear it.

Seeing how difficult it was to maintain a white sari, and how she felt about it, I once told her, 'Enough, Amma. You have worn this sari all these days. From now on, wear coloured ones.'

Perhaps wondering if I was saying this just to see how she would react, she looked at me carefully.

'I meant it, Amma.'

Now convinced, she said, 'If that mouth had said this on the day I was given the white sari, I could have worn coloured saris. But if I start wearing them now, after wearing white all these years, it will only set tongues wagging.'

I did not have the courage to confront the deep anguish her words revealed. I hung my head in shame. If only my father had lived a little longer, I wished, or at least that I had gained some worldly wisdom when he died. 'I lacked understanding then, Amma. Wear it now. Don't bother about what the others might say. How long will they talk, ten days? Let them. Or a month? Let them. They will soon find something else to talk about.'

Amma refused. 'I have worn it all these years. I am used to it. There's no need to change it now.'

I suggested that she go back to coloured saris on many occasions. But she always refused. Whenever we were buying clothes, I asked, 'Shall I buy a red sari, Amma?' She would brush it aside with a 'ptsch'.

I have regretted my lack of wisdom on many occasions. Later, when I knew better, I was able to set right some of my wrongs. But the white sari remained an issue I couldn't fix.

At any rate, in our family functions, Amma never hid in the back. My elder brother, his wife, my wife, all her grandchildren and I had enormous respect for her. We were bound by her strength and love. We wanted her to be at the forefront of every important occasion in the family and none of us had any issue with the omens of it. At our own family functions, rather than stay in the back, like she normally did at festive occasions, she chose to lead the ceremonies. This was a calculated choice and was triggered by an earlier event.

It was the month of Adi, mid-June to mid-July, a year after my father's death, the season for sowing maize. When he was alive, both Amma and Appa took on this task. The maize seeds would be placed in a basket and held in one hand. The seeds would be picked up with the other hand and thrown against the basket as the person walked. The maize would brush against the basket and land on the soil. Care should be taken not to damage them while throwing them against the basket. They also shouldn't fall too close to each other or they would grow in clumps. It was an art that had to be learnt slowly and required a great deal of patience.

The ritual in our region is that the first sowing must be done by a girl child. If a child was not available, a woman could do it, but not a widow. Amma tried to get hold of someone, but as it was the sowing season, no one was free to do it for us. People were tending to their own fields.

Also, we did not know exactly when the tractor would come. It was in high demand during the season. If the tractor was ploughing a certain field, the neighbours too would catch hold of it.

We couldn't sow before the field was ploughed; the two had to be done simultaneously. If the sowing happened before the ploughing, ants and birds could get to the seeds more easily. Also, the maize wouldn't sprout if the soil lost its moisture.

Amma and I went around asking just about everyone for help. But people were either busy or acting pricey.

Anticipating the arrival of the tractor, we took a sack full of seeds and the sowing basket to the field to wait there. We were yet to find someone to do the sowing. Amma had never scolded me like she did that day. 'What's the use of having two boys? One is always at the shop. The other is always sitting with his book spread out, addicted to reading. Is it not shameful that a farmer's sons do not know to sow maize?' This was the politest of her scoldings.

The tractor arrived. There was no one to sow and the tractor owner wouldn't wait until someone arrived. He was already asking us to hurry up.

Amma took handfuls of the seed, thrust them into my hands and asked me to sow. I was hesitant, but on seeing Amma's anger and hurry, I started sowing. Only, I sowed them in a clump. She tried to instruct me but I was too nervous to understand anything. The maize landed on the soil in all kinds of ways. After a point, she ran out of patience.

'Give it to me,' she said, grabbing the basket from me and placing it on the ground.

'O Mother, Kariyakali! You have to come reside in my hands and save us,' she prayed and then began sowing. I kept refilling the basket with seeds as it emptied. Amma did the sowing for all three acres.

Through the tractor driver, the story of Amma sowing the maize spread like wildfire in our village. For the next few days, even strangers dropped by to enquire. Women came home as if they were offering condolences. Several questions were posed: 'Whatever the case, is it right for you to do the sowing? Will the seeds sprout? Even if they do, will they ever reach the house?'

Amma had a different response for each question. She chased a few away with: 'If it has to sprout, it will sprout.

If it does not, let it go!' She tried to placate some with: 'Because I couldn't find anyone, I had to do the sowing myself,' or with: 'Even if I stay barren, the field should not. So I sowed.'

It rained heavily that year. Not a single maize crop that Amma sowed went bad. To describe it in Amma's words: 'The crop is lush. Not one is bare or infected. It's soothing to the eyes.'

Everything was smooth, even the harvest. When the crops reached home, Amma said, 'Goddess Kariyakali has proved that seeds will sprout even if a widow sows. That is enough.'

# 14

# A Ploughman's Accounts

It could be called a bet, or seen as an experiment.

Amma was constantly worried about our rain-fed land. She had various plans for the fields and lamented that my brother and I did nothing about it, while others in the village were trying out different things in agriculture.

'What do we get from farming? We don't even recover the investment,' I would tell her.

'You were born a farmer, how can you let the field lie fallow? How can you question what it gives us? Where does the food you eat and the clothes you wear come from? The money for your education comes from tilling this land. Does that education teach you this? If you work hard, Booma Devi will give in abundance. She won't deceive you. If you merely sit around doing nothing and staring at the land, she will only slap you across the face!' Amma would roast me.

It was 1987. I was a first-year post-graduate student and had come home for my study holidays in the second half of March. It rarely rains in the Tamil month of Panguni, mid-March to mid-April. But that year, it poured one night.

Our fields were flooded the next morning. The sun had lost all its strength and the temperature had cooled. As soon as Amma came back from surveying the fields, she began to rant. 'It has rained in the month of Panguni! The sight of the fields filled with water makes me yearn. In another four days, she would have drunk it all up. We have to sow before that. This is a good season to sow sesame. But what can a single woman do? What's the use of having two sons? There's no one to help me.'

Not able to bear Amma's rants, I retorted: 'Whether you sow sesame or horse gram, there's only loss. Somehow it has rained out of the blue. But how can we be sure that there will be more rains? If we sow and it doesn't rain, we'll lose everything.'

'You never have any good words to say, do you? The person who sows needs to have faith. It could be that there is no yield one year. But is that reason enough to be scared and not sow?' Amma scolded me.

Unable to argue any further, I relented. 'Fine, let it go. Why ruin your wish? Tell me what I should do.'

'A lean person will sow sesame and a fat person horse gram, goes an adage. No one has lost anything from sowing sesame.'

'Another adage says one must sow cautiously in Panguni. What do we do about that?'

'It simply means that we should sow only if it rains in Panguni.'

'Okay, Amma. We'll sow sesame and build a seven-storey building. Don't you worry!'

'This is a good season. My words will come true, you wait and watch. We will get some money in hand.'

Our conversation had transformed into something of a challenge. I maintained that we would not get anything even if we toiled hard, while Amma kept saying we would get everything. Finally we arrived at a decision: I would write down every expense from the cost of ploughing the field to labour, and after harvest, we would find out who was right. All Amma cared about was sowing.

We sowed sesame on one acre of land. We hired a tractor to plough the land twice. Since sesame seeds are tiny, they cannot be sown directly, or they will fall on the ground in clumps and grow too close together. This method also ended up using a much greater volume of seeds. Hence it was necessary to mix mud with the seeds, the ratio depending on their size, before sowing. The soil was still moist when we sowed. That very night, I made entries on tractor expenses, cost for seeds and the labour costs for Amma and myself.

Just as Amma had predicted, the sesame sprouted and grew well. I realised that the month of Panguni was indeed suitable for the crop. It was a delight to look at the plants in the morning light. Their dark green leaves danced in the wind and called out to us. Gazing at it gave us endless joy. 'The field is lush with sesame plants,' Amma said.

Although we had mixed the seeds with mud, they still sprouted in thick clusters. This was bad for the yield. Each plant needs enough space to branch out, feel the wind, and bloom. So when they grew to a cubit's length, the field had to be ploughed again.

Modern technology is sometimes incompatible with traditional farming practices. I came to realise this when it was time to plough again. We couldn't use a tractor; if its tyres trampled on the sesame plant, that would be the end of it. It didn't have the appropriate mechanism for ploughing at this stage. We searched for a person who used bulls for the job and hired him. This method would level the plants. Since there were only a couple of people who did the traditional kind of ploughing, his services came at a higher price than the tractor's.

I did not think this was a good idea. We could do the job ourselves by hand instead of taking on this unnecessary expense, I told Amma. But she argued that besides removing the unwanted plants, the ploughing would also loosen the soil and aid the remaining plants in putting down their roots better. As soon as the task was finished, I recorded how much it had cost us.

For some days in between, there were no rains. The plants began to wilt. Though I was sad, I also felt a cheap thrill at the possibility of winning against Amma. But soon, it rained again and my happiness was short-lived. The wilted plants blossomed with renewed energy. Grass too grew alongside, filling the fields. Amma and I cut the weeds. The grass that grew in thick clumps became fodder for the cows for a few days. The edible greens—pannai and kumutti—that we plucked along with the weeds were used for a kuzhambu a day. I calculated the labour cost for the weeding and put it down under the expenses column. Whenever I made entries in the accounts book, Amma laughed. But she didn't say anything.

The sesame plants bloomed and flourished. Each looked like a lamp with several wicks, fully lit up. They were now waist-high. Once again, we pulled out the weeds with our hands, without using a hoe. I recorded the labour cost for this as well.

As Amma had wished, it rained from time to time and disrupted my expectations. When the plants flowered, then became tender, ripe and finally mature, it was time to harvest them. We hoped for a mild shower. Harvesting sesame involved uprooting the plants by hand. If the soil was moist, it would be easier to pull them out. Otherwise, we would need to use a sickle, and that was a tough job. We waited for a few days for the rain to come. Thankfully, it did, and we began harvesting the very next day.

It took Amma and me two days to harvest one acre. We bundled up the harvested plants, tied them up and stacked them in the nearby rocky patch. We stacked three to four heaps and placed stones on them. They needed to be left out to dry for a week. Once the leaves fell off and only the sticks and fruits remained, we would have to separate each plant, allow it to dry some more, then thresh each of them separately against the rock for the sesame to fall off. It was a challenging task, but we pulled it off. I calculated the wages for that labour too and noted it down.

We transported the sesame to our house in gunny bags and baskets. Amma didn't want to sell it. She took a basket full of sesame to the oil press and brought back the extracted oil. The aroma of the fresh oil filled the house. We usually used only groundnut and castor oil for cooking. Now we cooked in the aromatic sesame oil.

One day, Amma pounded some sesame into flour, mixed it with palm jaggery and handed it to me. The taste of it would make you want to let it sit on the tongue forever and not swallow it at all. Another day, Amma made a thick gruel of split black gram, mixed it with sesame oil and served us. She said that it was good for the ribs. There was still some sesame left over, but Amma didn't sell that either. Had we incurred only expenses for this? Wasn't there going to be any income?

I often looked at the accounts notebook and kept asking Amma if we could tally it. She asked me to be patient.

A couple of people from the village came by and bought a padi of sesame, about 1.6 kilos, each. She enquired about the cost of sesame in the weekly market and took money from them accordingly. That was the only cash inflow.

Finally, Amma agreed to balance the accounts. I read it out delightedly and explained it to her. Traditional ploughing was the only expense we had paid for in cash. The rest was an account of our labour charges, Amma's and mine. The income part only listed the sesame sold the other day.

Amma said, 'Include whatever I say under income.'

I smiled and nodded, and Amma began.

'Add ten bundles of grass for the buffaloes. There might be more. But just put ten for now.'

'How much would they be?'

'Let's take care of the values later. For now, just put it under the income column.

'The sesame sticks can be used to heat water for a year. Write that down.

'Write seven measures of sesame oil. Then, seven big balls of sesame flour.

'We can use the leftover sesame to press more oil; add another seven measures.

'Then, if we had not sown and left the field fallow, what would we have done? We would have kept eating and sleeping at home. The sesame field gave us work. You have included the wages of two people on the expense side. That's wrong. Now, change it and write it under the income column. Let's take a look now.'

Looking up at her, I said, 'This is not acceptable at all, Amma.'

'If we had paid money for grass for the buffalo, the expenses would have doubled. You wrote ten bundles, didn't you?

You would have to make that twenty bundles to tally the accounts.'

'This is unfair, Amma. I don't agree!'

'Oh, what's unfair? An adage goes that if a farmer tallies his accounts, he won't even be left with a hoe! What does that mean? A farmer must not do accounts. What price will you fix for all this in your accounts? Didn't you go to the field every morning and roam around? Which account should we add it to?' Amma asked.

'You are cheating me, Amma! I won't agree to this!'

'Okay. If that is so, didn't you gobble up the greens and the gruel because they were so delicious? You said the kumitti smelled so good, poured it in your hands and licked it off. Do the math for all that or spit it all out!'

'Get lost, Amma. Do you think you understand accounts better than I do?'

'If you calculate the accounts for agricultural work, this is how it's going to be. Do you remember how the entire field was glowing in white when the sesame flowers bloomed? Let me see you put down a price for the joy you gained by merely looking at them!'

'Look, Amma. Only the money which we give out with our hands and that which comes into our hands are added to the accounts. Use these as guidelines to argue!' I disguised my helplessness in harsh words.

'Give me that accounts notebook,' she said and took it from me. She tore up the pages in which the entries were made and threw them into the stove burning nearby. The fire rose up in the air.

15

# 800 Square Feet

Amma always handled the family's finances, when my father was around and also after his death. In Amma's accounting, there was room only for income. The expense column was minimal; it was difficult to extract money from her, and she would hand it over only if she was fully convinced that it was necessary.

She enrolled in income-based chit fund schemes, usually run by men and largely populated by them too. Amma stood boldly among them and calculated with such impeccable clarity the taking of bids for a chit or the deduction of a chit amount that even the men were in awe of her. She also helped out those who didn't understand the nuances of the chit scheme, by calculating things like: the chit number currently under auction, the final amount after a deduction that they had agreed to, what the amount would be at an interest of 1 per cent or 2 per cent for the remaining months, whether or not it was profitable to deduct from the total amount and avail the rest of the money at a given point in time. She could calculate all of these precisely. Watching her, you had to wonder if even the person who ran the chit fund had such clarity. It was difficult to believe that Amma was familiar with such subtleties.

Little by little, she would build something new with the capital she accumulated like this. When Appa was alive, they bought five acres of land in three instalments of two, two and one. This was made possible only because of Amma's ability to save money. Although my father worked hard, he did not focus on saving any of it. When their savings reached a significant amount, Amma always wanted to invest in something. That is how they bought the land.

After my father's death, we had no income. Amma's earnings were just enough to meet my college expenses and support my brother and his family. There wasn't enough money for any major project. Amma would have been at peace if we managed to live on what we had. But we were not even capable of that. She had to watch as we were forced to sell two of our properties, and it caused her great heartache.

We had inherited an ancestral house built during the time of my paternal grandfather's father. That house was the result of my ancestors' hard work. There is a big story attached to it.

Those days, houses were normally built with mud. Some were constructed with a mixture of mud and gravel. Only the rich could afford brick houses. It was an extraordinary feat for an ordinary agrarian family to build such a house.

My ancestors had apparently established a brick kiln on their own land to build the house, and the red sand for the bricks too came from the land. They referred to this land as 'kuzhiyanappu'— hollowed out, because of the digging. The whole family was involved in the brick-making process, from cutting the stone to drying it to kindling the fire in the kiln. But nobody lived in the house for a long time. Since the family lived in the fields, the house was used to store grains.

Our family was the only one to live in it for a few years. It was a beautiful house. There were five wooden steps leading up to it from the ground. The entrance had a porch, and there was a veranda in which we could sit with our backs resting against it. The kitchen was set at a lower level and was spacious. There was also a big pattachalai, an outhouse of sorts, in which gifts from Amma's wedding trousseau, like a set of eleven stools and cupboards to store our clothes, were kept.

That house had been set aside for Appa and Amma when they were ready to start an independent family unit. This was where Amma started her life as a married woman. This was the house she delivered three babies in.

The roof had originally been built with handmade tiles of the olden days, which my parents later replaced with curvy red ones, called 'seemai tiles'. They also built a bathroom in the front. Amma vividly remembered every inch of that house long after we had moved out. Around the time I started running around and playing, we moved to the fields, but we still had the house. We lived there again for a few years when I was in my teens, so it has an important place in my memories too.

Even when our lives drove us to different places, we continued to keep the house. Eventually, we had to dispose of a property to clear the debts that had piled up. After concluding that none of us would live there again, we sold it to the tenants living there at the time. Amma's heart ached for that house for as long as she lived. She couldn't come to terms with the fact that the ancestral property had been sold off in her lifetime, in front of her very eyes. 'Would your father have let this happen were he alive? Would we have been in this situation?'

We were also forced to sell off two acres of the land that my father had bought. We had lived on that land for fifteen years in a thatched shed. Appuchi, Thatha, Paati and Appa, who were no longer with us, had lived with us on that land. Amma had lived all by herself in that shed for some years, when my elder brother and family shifted to his mother-in-law's house after his marriage, and I moved to different cities to pursue my education. She didn't want to sell the land. However, when my brother committed suicide because of financial difficulties, we were left with no option but to sell it to clear his debts. Realising that this was our only option, she eventually agreed to sell it.

Remembering my father, she often said, 'He had bought this land, now we are selling it.'

We sold it for a very low price, and within a year of the sale, its value increased manifold. 'We should have gritted our teeth and held on to the land,' she said. Whenever Amma passed by the land, she stumbled over her memories and her eyes welled up. 'Let it go, Amma,' I would comfort her. 'Let's look at what we still have.'

Though we were forced to sell those two properties, Amma felt a sense of achievement and pride at having managed to retain a piece of land she had bought with her own earnings, after many obstacles.

When a land adjoining one of ours was partitioned, our house lost its entrance, and we had no say in the matter. It was only four feet from the house, but it was on not on our share of land any more and we could no longer use it. To access the common road, we had to go around the side of the house. Amma was filled with grief at the sight of a house without an entrance.

After the partition, the other landowners plotted up some of their land for sale. This included an 800-square-foot strip in front of our house. If we could purchase that, we would have a proper entrance again. We could also use the 30-foot path running through the plot to get to the road. Amma tried her best to buy the plot. Knowing that we would somehow buy it, the sellers increased the price. Amma found it hard to raise that money, and she was also against paying an unfair and exorbitant amount.

The talks failed. Amma told the sellers that she would sell her house to anyone who bought the plot of 800 square feet that stretched like a tail in front of our house. 'Where will that bit of land go? At some point, it will come back to us,' she often said.

All their plots were sold. Only a few that were further in and the strip in front of our house remained. A few years passed by. Amma began to use that tail-like piece of land. If the plot-owners saw her during an occasional visit, they would say, 'What is this, Amma. You are using our land?' To which she would say: 'I was merely washing a couple of utensils here. You may fence your land if you like.'

When the shareholders of the land split up, that strip-like plot, along with some others, went to a person who was broke. He offered that 800 square feet to Amma. She negotiated with him and bought it.

Our finances were in bad shape at that time. There was hardly any income. When one of the two buffaloes calved and was yielding milk, the other was pregnant. Our family lived off the milk of one buffalo. I was studying and my elder brother, who had two children, was unemployed. We also had a few goats. I wondered how Amma managed to save any money under these circumstances. She probably used the money from the buffalo milk for household expenses and saved the money from the sale of goat kids.

When I asked, she said, 'I wake up in the middle of the night and secretly mint notes.' Sometimes she would say, 'If you climb the almond tree at the entrance and shake it, money will fall!' Once she said, 'Your father had buried it under the stove!' and laughed. But somehow she managed to save money and buy that 800 square feet of land.

Not long before this, she had tripped and fallen, and thousands of rupees had to be spent on her treatment. This too came from her savings. Yet, there was money to buy the plot after this expenditure, and it was a big achievement in Amma's life. Talking about it made her happy—not only because the property was bought with her savings but also because the house now finally had an entrance.

When our family properties were divided between my elder brother and I, I got the house. Every time Amma had an argument with me, she would say: 'Even when I was bedridden after falling down, I still managed to buy an entrance for your house!'

That would make me laugh. 'Yes, Amma! Did I ever deny it?'

'If you remember it, then all right.'

Even today, when I set foot on that entrance, I am reminded of Amma and the feat she accomplished.

# 16

# A Long Journey

Amma hardly ever travelled, and had only been as far as the villages around ours and the city nearby. As far as I know, she had also made a trip to Palani—which the people in our village considered a long journey—three or four times.

There was a pending votive offering to have my head tonsured at Palani. It was necessary for the entire family to visit the temple when fulfilling a vow to tonsure a family member's head. We couldn't find time for it, though. Appa, who had made monthly visits to Palani to pray for a second child, went there only on occasions like Thai Poosam and Panguni Utthiram once I was born.

My hair would be allowed to grow out in the hope of getting me tonsured in Palani, and then we wouldn't be able to go. Instead, I was tonsured at local temples where we had made similar vows. In the course of a few years, I had my head tonsured on many occasions. If I suffered from an infestation of lice, I was taken to whichever temple was going to have its festival soon and my hair was shaved off. I have offered my hair to several female deities like Mariamman, Kaliamman and Selliamman, and a few times to the male deities Muniappan, Murugan and Perumal.

My hair used to be so long that it had to be braided. Since I was the same age as my uncle's daughters, Amma dressed me up like them, braiding my hair and applying talcum powder on my face. I took a liking to it. If I spotted a cousin with a plait, I would run to Amma and demand that she braid my hair right away. She would gather up the middle portion of my hair at the front and braid it. I only occasionally sported a single plait, because I preferred double plaits and that was what I almost always wore. Amma would gently part my hair like flowers, braid it and adorn it with ribbons.

Holding up my plaits, like they were the horns of a goat, I would butt Amma with my head. Pretending to be scared, she would scream, 'Ayyo! This wild goat has come to butt me. Someone please come and catch him!' and laugh heartily. We called this the game of the plaits. Sometimes, she was busy when I wanted to play. If I went ahead and butted her anyway, she would scold me, 'You will grow some brains only when we shave off all your hair.'

I didn't like having my head tonsured. The boys had a game called the bald-head game, which involved sneaking up and touching or stroking a boy's bald head and then running off, only to stop and sing a mocking song:

> Is it a tonsured head?
> or baldness that has just sprouted?
> Will you come to pluck flowers?
> I will not,
> I am scared of a fox.

Girls were not spared this cruel song either. Scared that my head would become a playing field, I would get angry and cry each time Amma mentioned tonsuring. Moved by my tears, she would put aside all her work and attend to me. 'Look at that wild goat charging towards me with its horns raised. Someone save me!' I would immediately stop crying and turn into a goat.

I also played with the goat kids using my pretend horns, challenging them to a fight. During these times, I turned into an actual goat. I loved the way goat kids leapt into the air or hopped across pits or skipped as they ran. I often regretted not having been born a goat.

Face powder came to the villages in the 1960s. When a girl attained puberty, she would be gifted at least one box of face powder. People took pride in having it in their house and we too had one. After braiding my hair, Amma would apply powder on my face and stick a pottu on my forehead. It looked like my face was plastered with ash, but also beautiful. Amma would place a big black dot on my cheek to ward off evil eyes. When I insisted that it had to be a perfect circle, she would say that it was not meant to be, even as she continued to adjust it. I also threw tantrums, demanding that she apply kohl on my eyes. Sometimes she did that too. It probably helped satiate her yearning for a girl child. A girl child could help sweep the entrance or do the dishes.

I was still wearing plaits when I joined school. The boys pulled my plaits and called me a girl. When I went to pee, the older boys troubled me by undoing my ribbons. I would return to class in tears. Since my class one teacher, Padma, had relatives in our village, she knew Amma rather well. She would call me to her sympathetically, wipe my tears and redo the ribbons.

Because of all this, I often refused to go to school. One day, when I was crying uncontrollably because of the bullying, Padma teacher told my brother, who was in class five then, that I should either have my hair shaved off or cut short. 'Tell your mother I said so,' she told him.

Left with no option, we started for Palani early one morning, leaving the goats and cows in my grandmother's care for a day. We had to go to Erode and then through Dharapuram and Kangeyam, which were rain-fed farming areas. 'I thought that our village was parched. But the way to Palani is worse!' Amma remarked.

There were only a few buses to Palani and it was difficult to get seats in them. There was always a crowd going to the temple waiting at the Erode bus stand. Amma and I had never gone to Palani before. After this, Appa and I made several trips there, and Amma probably joined us a couple of times.

Both Anna and I had our heads tonsured, and since the number of people offering their hair had to be in odd numbers, Amma offered up hers too. She placed a flower on her hair and donated the part below it.

On our way up, Appa took us along a path used by elephants, and on our way back, he took us down the steps. 'This is smaller than the hill in our village. But it has two paths. It would be nice to have a path like this on our hill too,' Amma said.

The issue of tonsuring my head ended there.

Apart from this, Amma had travelled to Erode, about twelve miles from home. It was customary for people from our area to buy clothes from there for weddings. Amma went to Erode several times to shop for weddings in the family and also thrice for Appa's surgeries. And each time, she made some remark or the other on the river Kaveri that runs through the city. 'This river has only as much water as the smaller streams in our village.' 'Oh my, the water is overflowing on both the banks!' 'We are being supplied ditch water in the name of river water and this is what we gulp down!' Amma loved looking at the river while crossing the bridge, soon after the bus passed Pallipalayam.

The other place she visited was Pachaperumalpatti near Thorayur in Trichy district, where her uncle and his family lived, to attend a few weddings and funerals. She and I had gone there to invite our relatives for my brother's wedding too. One had to cross Namakkal to reach Pachaperumalpatti. After my wife and I shifted to Namakkal, Amma visited us several times. She had no problem travelling on the bus by herself. Each time, she got off the bus at Namakkal and walked the mile's distance to our house, never taking the local bus. 'Can't I walk even this distance? Do I have to part with two rupees for this? Anyway, I would rather walk a few steps than go through the hassle of waiting for a bus, then boarding it and getting off it.' When Amma fell ill, someone would accompany her to the bus in the village and I received her at the Namakkal bus stand.

These were her journeys. Although the word 'journey' might be an exaggeration.

I had often asked Amma to visit Chennai when I was a student there, and later when I lived there with my wife. But she never came. Though she wished to see the sea and

I had so wanted to show her around the city, she refused to come, using the goats and buffaloes as an excuse. Then, her ill health became an excuse. 'Will looking at the sea fill my stomach?' was her usual retort.

Though my father-in-law's family belonged to Ranipet in Vellore district, since I got married while studying in Chennai, Amma considered Chennai as my father-in-law's place.

'He was married in Madras,' she told those who enquired. I invited her to visit my wife's house when I got married, but Amma refused, so instead I took a few relatives with me. She didn't attend my wedding either.

Given the circumstances then, I couldn't invite anyone from my father-in-law's family to our home. They sent off their daughter with me and could not even accompany her to her new home. Nearly a decade later, my mother-in-law visited our village once and stayed with us for a few days. But my father-in-law never could visit us to see the village his daughter was married into or the state of his son-in-law's house. He had always wanted to come, and when the time and circumstances were finally right, he fell ill. But because of him, my mother made another journey

Amma was bedridden after a fall, and I looked after her for a month in the hospital. When she came home, I had to stay and care for her for a few more months. Though my brother's house was close by, Amma didn't want to go there. Since his daughter and son were in school, it was difficult for my sister-in-law to visit Amma. So my wife stayed with us and took care of her. My daughter was a year old then, and my wife was pregnant for the second time. Amma was moved that my wife had stayed behind despite this.

Amma thought that she had lost her son when I got married in Madras, fearing that I wouldn't visit her anymore. But on seeing how we took care of her, she began to think that all was not lost. Some friends and relatives had told her after my marriage, 'He will now live in his father-in-law's house. Why would an educated boy come and live with us here?' As the exact opposite had come to pass, Amma was touched.

Later, when I got a job in a government college, we returned to our village and lived with my mother for a few years. It further strengthened Amma's belief that her son had not strayed far from her after all. Perhaps, that's why she volunteered to visit my father-in-law when he fell ill. 'I must visit him once. Will you take me?' she asked. We were very happy to hear this.

On a holiday, my wife accompanied Amma to Ranipet and I stayed back home to look after the children. That was her longest journey. They had to take a bus to Erode, then board a train from there to Katpadi, and board another bus from there to Ranipet—a seven- to eight-hour trip. Despite not being well enough to travel by bus for long stretches, Amma decided to travel.

Since part of it was on a train, she was able to manage. Back then, it was difficult to make a reservation in advance on trains. One had to go to the railway station in Erode at a given time, stand in a queue and buy a ticket. The trip to secure a seat alone took half a day. So rather than booking tickets in advance, we usually travelled by the day train that had unreserved compartments. This is what Amma did too.

However, the two of them couldn't find a seat in the unreserved compartment. My wife worried about Amma having to stand all the way. 'It's not a problem, I can manage,' Amma told her. Those who had found seats would initially be unwilling to share, but once the train moved, they felt bad for the others and accommodated them too. A space meant for four was usually occupied by five or even six people. This is how Amma got a place to sit. She enjoyed observing her co-passengers during the journey.

Apparently, in the course of a conversation, a co-passenger had said, 'You will know if you visit Aayipalayathan's house; you will know if you lived there for two days.' Relatives might boastfully claim many things about themselves, but to know who they really are, you need to visit them. This is was what the proverb meant. Amma burst out laughing on hearing this, but my wife could neither understand the proverb nor the reason for her sudden laughter. It was the first time Amma was visiting my in-laws' home and she had probably been thinking about how it would turn out. She might have laughed because a random proverb had unexpectedly reflected her thoughts.

In keeping with the proverb, Amma not only visited my in-laws' house but also stayed there for two days. They had arranged for a cot and mattress for her to sleep on. She was surprised that everyone, except my father-in-law, slept on the floor. In our village, each person had their own coir cot, and people rarely slept on the floor.

They served her idli and mutton kuzhambu for breakfast the next morning. Amma told them that she really liked it. 'We'd grind and add dry coriander seeds, which was missing. But otherwise, it was nice!' was her final verdict.

Amma was happy to have finally met my in-laws. Having neither attended our wedding nor called on us when we had our first child, she probably felt that she had wronged us. But I never once forced her to visit our home. I presume she undertook that journey to my in-laws' place to atone for her mistakes.

She strengthened the bond with my wife's family by being at ease with them. Her visit made my father-in-law happy as well. It also signified Amma's approval of our marriage. That journey continued to be talked about by both sides of the family for some time after. That was also Amma's first train ride. A journey contains many things within it.

# 17

# The Walking Stick

I have observed many people involved in farming, and most of them have short lifespans. They succumb to depression after crossing fifty. Once their children grow up and take over the family work, they tend to feel irrelevant. This affects their physical health too and probably takes away a few years from their lives. The fatigue and stress caused by unending work is another factor.

There was no chance that Amma felt that her relevance had decreased. She continued to be responsible for our land and house. Since my brother and I took up jobs away from the field, we didn't diminish her sense of ownership. While she continued to take care of ploughing the land, sowing and harvesting, we only assisted her a little here and there, and never asked her about income or expenditure. Though Amma volunteered this information to us, we never paid it any attention. For many years, she even managed our personal accounts. We didn't do anything that would dent Amma's relevance in our home. In fact, we only tried to add to it, and she was satisfied on this account.

It was the second problem, fatigue, that haunted Amma. After her fall, she couldn't work the way she used to. A few years later, she was affected by Parkinson's disease, which drastically reduced her ability to work. She was unable to accept that she could no longer work like before and repeatedly tried to get back to her old routines. When she failed, it not only saddened her but also affected her mental health. Let me give you an example.

It was the season for harvesting groundnuts. I had gone to see Amma during the day. She was not at home and there was no one else around either. Assuming that she would be in the fields, I went in search of her. On the way, I met someone and asked him about Amma. 'What could possibly happen to your mother who is competing with young girls in harvesting the groundnuts. Take a look yourself', he said.

Shocked, I went to the fields. Sitting in front of creepers she had cut with a hoe, Amma was busy plucking out the nuts. A cloth was wrapped around her head as protection from the sun and she was covered in red earth.

'What is all this, Amma?' I asked.

Reading my face, she tried to console me. 'I am all right, so I thought I could do this instead of sitting idle. If I am unable to, I will go back.'

I was too angry to respond. So, she followed me home. At that time, Amma had just begun to take medicines for an ache in her arms and legs. The doctor had advised her to handle only light chores. Amma had the habit of taking on work the moment her health improved a little, eventually making it worse.

It wasn't just that she was unable to make peace with not being able to work; it was also that Amma believed she could do nothing else. She wasn't interested in anything apart from her work either. The elderly living in cities can find various activities to engage in. I tried my best to push Amma towards taking up some hobby or the other. But our cities and villages have very little by way of recreation. There are no public places one can visit, barring cinema theatres. Nor are there any parks or playgrounds, and the rare music concert or public speech happens only during temple festivals. Moreover, Amma was not interested in any of these either. She did watch movies for some time and TV serials too but nothing suited her disposition.

To keep her occupied, I suggested that she visit the temple once or twice a week. There was a Mariamman temple in the village, with benches outside for people to sit on. She might run into a few people there. It wasn't very far and she could easily make that trip. There were several small temples near our home in Namakkal, and about half a furlong away, there was a big temple where poosai and distribution of food to the poor took place every day. I even offered to accompany her. Once she got used to going, she wouldn't need a companion anymore, or she might find new ones, I thought.

Though Amma believed in god, she wasn't in the habit of going to temples. During temple festivals, she would go with us to offer pongal or sacrifice goats and hens. But she didn't go on other days.

A temple isn't just a place of worship but also a public place to meet people and forge friendships. It is a good place to pass time without spending money. I tried convincing Amma to visit one regularly, but she would have none of it. 'Should I go to the temple at this age and ask god to grant me boons? Women who sit idle gorging on food and putting on weight visit temples because they have nothing else to do. Do you want me to sit and exchange stories with them?' These were her standard responses to my entreaties.

Once, I responded unthinkingly, 'What work do you have here, anyway?'

'Do you mean to say I sit around doing nothing and just eat?' she asked angrily.

I quit trying after that.

Amma never considered adapting her everyday life to suit her age and health. I wondered if she would have been in better health if she had spent her old age around her grandchildren. But they were all grown up and studying in schools or colleges, and couldn't spend time with their grandmother. They did attend to her when they were home, but that wasn't enough. How could we possibly let her work like she used to?

Another example of how she felt about her situation comes to mind.

In 2010, I went to South Korea for a writers' conference. Since that was my first trip abroad, I had to buy gifts for friends and family. I have never been interested in material things and always think many times over before buying something. I wonder if the item is necessary at all. Even if I conclude that it is, I give myself some time to see if I can manage without it before actually making the purchase. I am, therefore, no expert on gifts.

So when I went shopping in South Korea, I had no idea what people needed or liked, and tied myself up in knots choosing the gifts. I obsessed over the difference between what it cost here and what it would cost back home. With the help of a woman who was sent to assist me, I managed to buy some things. But I was still confused about what to get for Amma.

I had never bought anything significant for her. She never seemed to need anything. By the time I could afford gifts for her, she had become a widow. I couldn't buy clothes for someone who only wore white saris. Neither could I buy jewellery for someone who left her hands, neck and ears bare. I haven't bought her many utensils or other household items. Even if I had, they were not something she could flaunt.

Fundamentally, the human race needs very little. People started developing needs only after the spread of the consumerist culture. Amma was representative of an era untouched by consumerism, and so I really couldn't think of anything for her. Resolving that I would give her something from what I had already bought, I returned to Namakkal. She was back in the village then.

I had to visit the Sarvodaya Sangha store before I met Amma. They had some beautiful walking sticks on display. Amma had been finding it difficult to walk. On the way to the field, she sometimes picked up a branch and used it to maintain her balance. In the old films, the rich always had a walking stick and it seemed like a symbol of wealth. In many of them, S.V. Ranga Rao carried a stick and even twirled it. The ones in the movies always had comfortable curvy handles. When I saw a similar one in the store with a beautifully carved handle, I decided to buy it for Amma.

When I gave it to her, her face initially betrayed no expression. 'I have grown old. So, you bought me a walking stick to suggest that I use one?' she asked.

She looked at the walking stick in disgust and I could almost physically feel it.

'What happened, Amma. Don't you like it?'

'I like it all right. I'll use it to go to the field to remove weeds.'

Had I encouraged Amma to go to the field to cut weeds? I was quiet.

I shouldn't have bought her the walking stick. An act of empathy based on a person's age transforms ageing into a disability. The walking stick was a symbol of disability. She wouldn't have anticipated that this is what her foreign-returned son would bring her. What could she have expected, though? I never spoke to her about the walking stick after that.

One day, she said, 'Paiya, the walking stick is a little too tall.' It was obvious that she had tried using it.

'We can cut it at the base,' I told her.

Amma was very short and her head and shoulders looked like they were stuck together. Perhaps she would have looked taller had her neck been a little longer. After her fall, when she hit her head against a rock, her neck shrank further and made her appear even smaller.

But I have never seen Amma use that stick. I had no idea what she did with it or where she kept it. I used to wonder whether she had got rid of it, but she is not the kind to throw things away. Then I discovered it by accident one day. While I was rummaging through some things piled up in the shed, I spotted the gleaming walking stick stuffed into the thatch.

# 18

# A Life Bestowed by Trees

Amma always had money on her. She never expected anything from anyone for her needs. Even when her health deteriorated, she sold all the goats and cows and confined herself to the house. The two-room house in the fields, in which I used to live with my family, was lying vacant after we moved to Namakkal. We told Amma to move there, but she decided she didn't need such a large house and rented it out. There was a small room behind the house where my books were stored. She told us that this ten-by-ten room with its roof made of handmade tiles was all she needed.

Refusing to take any money that I offered her, she would ask, 'What expenses do I have?' Instead, she always sent off her visiting grandchildren with a gift of ten or twenty rupees.

The rent she received from the house was around a hundred to hundred and fifty rupees. Even though she was living by herself, how could that possibly suffice? I used to take her some vegetables and provisions when I visited her. This made Amma angry. 'Why do I need all this? What am I going to do with it? Why do you waste money? I'll ask you if I need anything.' So I made a habit of first checking if she needed anything and bought only the things that she requested. When I asked her how she manages her expenses, she pointed to the trees outside and said, 'They give me.' Yes, the income from a few trees was enough for her.

Amma didn't know any agricultural work before her marriage, but once she learnt it, even the way she grew a plant was tasteful. There was always a chilli plant near the area where she washed vessels. That single plant took care of a year's supply of chillies for her, and would survive for two to three years. Branching out like a green umbrella with a broad base, it was also soothing to look at. She plucked the fresh green chillies, of course, but she also allowed them to ripen, then dried and preserved them. One or two sunberry plants were good enough to make a poriyal once every ten days. The ways in which Amma made use of nature was fascinating.

Even in our house at Namakkal, she nurtured some trees. She planted a drumstick tree and a curry leaf plant on the street, right next to our wall, and tended to them so that they reached our terrace from where we could pluck the produce for our use. The henna plant that she grew in front of our house has today become a tree with branches spread out over our wall. Whenever I smell the fragrance of its flowers that wreathe our entrance, I am gripped by memories of Amma, of her planting and nurturing each of them with care.

Back in our village too, Amma had grown a few trees around our house and on our land. One each of curry leaf, drumstick, citron, guava, country gooseberry, and two each of mango, coconut, pomegranate and tamarind—there were thirteen trees in all.

The two tamarind trees were unique—their fruit didn't fall off even after they dried up; you had to hit with a stick to bring them down. Amma named them 'narambu puli' or nerve tamarind, because like nerves, they held on tightly and were difficult to cut off. She brought down each dried tamarind with a stick, and de-seeded and stored them. Setting aside enough for herself, she would give me and my brother a year's supply. The produce of the tamarind trees were not sold—the remaining eleven trees were Amma's source of income.

There were hardly any curry leaf plants in our area as water scarcity made it difficult to maintain the plant. It was considered such a miracle to spot even one that, in our parts, a single child was lovingly referred to as a tender curry leaf sprig. Amma placed a pot under her curry plant and filled it up whenever there was water in the tap. We used this to wash our hands and feet, and that was enough water for the plant. There was also a pot each beneath the two coconut trees. Amma washed utensils there, so there was no need to separately water the coconut trees either. The guava and gooseberry trees in front of her small room shaded the entrance to the house, and they only needed a little water every now and then.

The two pomegranate trees stood in the gap between the house and the pathway to the road. My wife had germinated a few seeds in a polythene bag and then transplanted them there. But the moment the pomegranate bloomed and started fruiting, worms would suddenly appear out of nowhere and ruin them. Amma tried smearing ash on the unripe fruit, but the worms managed to eat through and digest the ash.

Once, she covered the fruit with a small polythene bag lying around the house and tied it up with a thread. The worms couldn't tear through it, and polythene bags came to serve as pesticide. From then on, Amma kept an eye on the tree and pounced to wrap a polythene bag around the fruit as soon as it made an appearance, before the worms could get to it. It looked like polythene bags were growing on the pomegranate tree. Occasionally, she removed the bags, aired out the fruit and then retied them. She only plucked the fruits when they were very ripe and came off easily so as not to hurt the tree. Selling the fruits that remained after we had our share brought in good money.

The occasional rains served the henna and drumstick tree. Henna had no commercial value, so if a person buying something else wished to take some, Amma let them. The drumstick tree yielded something or the other all year long. Its greens were perennial and dreadlocks of drumsticks hung from the tree during the season. Amma had acquired the skill of plucking the vegetable without breaking the delicate branch, and she never let anyone else do the job. When the branches broke off in the wind, she grieved as if her own arm had broken. The drumstick needs the sort of attention that children with special needs do, and that is exactly how Amma took care of her tree. The two mango trees were in the field, away from the house, and she had a long hose to water them.

Amma did not waste anything her trees offered. She never went to the market empty-handed, always carrying with her two or three bunches of curry leaves or drumstick leaves or some vegetables in a bag. They would get sold to houses on the way. Young boys came home in search of guavas and gooseberries. Since Amma couldn't reach them, she let whoever came for them pluck the fruit and took whatever money they offered. During the mango season, she guarded the trees throughout the day. If she spotted even a shadow near the trees, Amma would ask sternly, 'Who's there?'

When she left our home after a visit, Amma plucked any extra drumsticks and leaves to sell them on her way back, ensuring that nothing was wasted.

Not even a tiny tender fruit could escape Amma's sharp eye or leave her territory without her knowledge. She refused to visit us during the mango season, no matter how much we begged her to. And when she did, she would come in the evening and leave early the next morning. When we visited her, she would immediately walk to the trees and come back with a couple of mangoes that had already ripened on the tree. Handing the fruits to us, she would say, 'I let them be on the tree because you were coming,' as if she had sought the tree's permission to let the fruit stay there longer. We also always got well-ripened guavas and gooseberries. Amma knew every inch of the trees.

During mango season, Amma's cash inflow was good. She also sold coconuts. What income did she get from these sales? A few hundred rupees. Three hundred rupees a month was more than enough for her, and she would even save some. I estimated that, including the house rent, Amma got a maximum of five hundred rupees every month. She managed to buy rice, lentils, vegetables and provisions with that money.

She knew that I had a well-paying government job. I was willing to take care of all her needs and she was proud of it. Stories of children letting their elderly parents struggle for food were common in the village. Society believes that we must have children so they can care for us in our old age, when we should not be working. Parents and others often coo to baby boys, 'Won't you take care of your father and mother when they become old?' But very many children abandon their parents. Though Amma did fear such a thing in the beginning, she soon overcame it. My actions had instilled confidence in her.

To those who asked her if I was taking care of her, she said, 'Will he ever say he will not give me something? He offers me wads of notes. I am the one who refuses them. Does he come empty-handed to see me? He brings bags full of all sorts of useless things. Are there any children here to use them? I tell him not to bother. Aren't these trees enough for a single person?'

Amma lived for eight years after she was diagnosed with Parkinson's. Though she took homeopathy medicine, on the advice of the homeopath, she also took an allopathy tablet every day. It was an expensive pill. Worried that she would refuse to take them if she knew their price, I always told her it cost much less. I bought her the tablets every month without fail. When someone in the village asked her, 'You educated your boy, didn't you? Does he take care of you?' she would say, 'Can't you see how he's flooding me with tablets every month? Does he ever clearly say how much he spends on them? Perhaps they cost a thousand or even two thousand rupees. Who knows.'

The trees were more than a source of income for Amma and did her another big favour.

Whenever I visited, I would find her sitting or standing under a tree. Our house was isolated. The other houses were within calling distance, but one didn't see passersby often. Even if we saw someone occasionally, the conversation would only last a few seconds. Everyone had their own work to attend to. The trees kept Amma company. She talked to them. She was one with them. She noticed the smallest of changes in them. She knew exactly how many tender fruits were on each tree, how many unripe ones and how long it would take for them to ripen. The trees lent their ears to her. Thanks to them, Amma's lifespan increased by a few years.

For two years, the rains failed and there was seldom any water in the tap at home. Amma struggled to save the trees. Because of the Parkinson's, she couldn't stretch her hands and legs properly or lift heavy objects. The trees in the vicinity of the house posed no major problem, but the mango trees were wilting. She was desperate to save them and bought two toy pots that children played with. These she filled with water and walked to the mango trees, stopping a couple of times in between to regain her strength. Amma watered the trees every day in this manner and nursed them back to health.

Her only request when we called on her was: 'Pour a pot of water for that mango tree before leaving.' She requested the same of those who came to buy something too. The mango trees didn't bloom for two years. But they held on to their lives because Amma watered them. In the third year, there was some rain, and the mango trees flowered and yielded fruit. Amma's joy knew no bounds.

Her final year was very difficult. Given her worsening health condition, she had to come live with us. To any visitor from the village, she first enquired after her trees. We also made it a point to water the trees whenever we visited. On the days she felt better, Amma would stubbornly insist we put her on a bus to our village. She stayed for at least a week, watering the trees with her small water pots throughout her stay. Amma was deeply saddened that there was no one to look after them.

In the last six months, she couldn't visit her house, and we watered the trees each time we went there. That was all we could do. It was difficult to water trees that were twenty-five miles away even once a month. After Amma passed away, we couldn't go there for a few months. When I finally visited her house to clear out her belongings, I wanted to see the trees. There isn't much to say about them. The two mango trees had dried up and stood like bare poles—the fate of orphaned kids.

## 19

# THE GOLDEN POT

Amma had very few needs. As a young woman, she only wore a single neck-hugging gold chain of three sovereigns and a pair of earrings with white stones. Appuchi gave her these for her wedding.

Afterwards, she only wore the yellow auspicious thread of a married woman around her neck. If the thread wore off, she would be bare-necked for some time. Where did she have the time to take care of all this in the middle of all her work in our fields? Only when someone pointed out, 'You're a married woman, how can you walk about bare-necked?' would she remember to replace the thread. Later, when she found the time, she would take a piece of thread, fold it twice or thrice over, smear turmeric on it and tie it around her neck. To prevent the piercing in her ears from closing up, she inserted twigs in them.

When Appa had saved some money from his shop at the cinema theatre, Amma got a thali chain of seven sovereigns made. Only then did it occur to me that perhaps Amma had wanted to wear a thali chain.

These were the only three ornaments she decked up in even when going to functions. She had one silk sari, which was bought during her wedding. I have never seen her wear the sari, which was spread out at the base of a storage box. The five or six cotton saris that were meant for her everyday use she bought at the market. When Amma was at home or in the fields, even my father's torn lungis would serve to cover her chest. She tied a cloth over her petticoat and blouse while working and that was all she needed.

After my father's death, Amma wore no jewellery or colourful saris. She had five or six white saris, which she rarely wore, and she wouldn't allow us to buy her saris on festivals like Diwali or Pongal. 'I don't even wear what I have. What'll I do with new ones other than letting them lie unused in a box?'

When I was a young boy, Amma used to have a sauri; those days, it was common for women to use such hair extensions for braiding their hair or making a bun. In fact, there was a shop in the market that exclusively sold these hair extensions. Amma never braided her hair, but she made a bun with the hair extensions and pinned it up with a long hairpin. The sauri too vanished over the years. I don't think Amma was interested in clothes and jewellery.

If there was one thing she was obsessed with, it was kitchen utensils. Though we didn't have the money, it was necessary to buy utensils for storing water and cooking, and also bigger ones for functions when we needed to cook for a large number of people. Besides using our own utensils, we also borrowed from relatives and neighbours. Borrowing came with its own set of problems—cheating the lender out of them, a couple of missing items, taking a long time to return them, etc. Moreover, while returning a utensil, there would be complaints like, 'It's dented,' 'It's not been washed properly,' 'The alloy has eroded,' and so on. This has damaged many relationships. People tried to wriggle out of this situation by claiming they didn't have the utensil even if they did.

Amma had two vessels with tapered bottoms to cook pongal in. One of them was very small, the other slightly bigger. Once, when we had to make an offering of a goat during the Mariamman temple festival, we invited more relatives than usual. Since we had to serve all of them pongal, we needed a big pot to cook in. Amma asked whoever she could, but all of them either said they didn't have one or that they needed it for their own use. So Amma cooked pongal in both pots, and when that wasn't sufficient, she cooked some more at home in an aluminium pot. Over the next few months, she somehow saved money and bought a big pot that could hold two measures of rice.

Amma only bought utensils that were essential. Her aesthetic preferences showed in the small vessels she bought. If there were ten tumblers, each one would be a different shape. She used every vessel for a different purpose based on its design. Her most preferred vessels were those that were variously curved. If ten or fifteen of them were waiting to be washed, they would all shine in different shapes.

Even the earthen pots that we used to have earlier were tastefully chosen. She used a range of utensils made of mud, aluminium, brass, copper, stainless steel and plastic. But she was especially fond of buying and caring for brass utensils. Perhaps she preferred them because they were a status symbol.

Just as there is a backstory for every literary character, each of her utensils too had a history. If we stepped out of the house with the copper sombu in hand, Amma would follow us out and take it back inside as soon as we finished drinking from it, claiming that we would leave it lying around outside. Appuchi had bought the sombu from Tirupati the one time he had gone there and it had paintings on the outside. Amma protected this little waterpot-shaped jug as if it were a wonder.

A plate, a tumbler, no matter how small the utensil was, Amma had a story for each of them. They were full of detail too, including where and when they were bought and how much they had cost. She knew every utensil at home, and if one them went missing, she couldn't focus on anything else until it was found. An entire loft in the kitchen was filled with brass utensils collected in various ways. Every summer, she brought these down from the loft, washed them with tamarind, dried them and then put them back gain, a tedious and time-consuming process.

Those who saw her collection asked, 'Do you have girl children that you have collected so many vessels?' It was customary to send utensils as part of a daughter's wedding trousseau. People usually collected the brass over time as it was expensive to buy them all at one go for the wedding. Though both her children were boys, Amma still had a large collection.

Her utensils posed a major problem when Amma decided to live in the small room adjoining our house. Though her heart wouldn't allow it, seeing no other way, she divided the vessels equally between Anna's family and mine. We made no claims over any particular vessel, and Amma was satisfied that she was able to divide it between us without any bias. We were not too keen on those utensils because our needs had changed, and vessels compatible with gas stoves were available. Moreover, what was one to do with huge vessels? People no longer cooked at home for a function, ordering from restaurants instead. Even if one had to cook, utensils were easily available on rent. If anything, they were a nuisance, taking up too much space, but since Amma was giving them to us, we accepted them without any complaints.

She didn't stop with giving away her vessels. An important task of hers was to survey them whenever she visited our homes. The way she monitored our upkeep and use of them was entertaining to watch.

Once, she saw a plate she had given my sister-in-law lying outside, and picked a fight with her. 'Is this how you throw the plate about? Do you even know when it was bought?' She believed that Anni couldn't maintain them responsibly.

Unable to take Amma's interference, Anni told her, 'I don't want a single thing from you. Please take them back.'

Using that as an excuse, one by one Amma brought back all the vessels she had given my brother. She requested the tenants to allow her the use of one loft, and stored the vessels there, covering them carefully with old saris and blankets.

When Anna's daughter got married a few years later, Amma gave all those vessels to her. The groom's family was from an agrarian community, and came in a bullock cart to pick them up. Amma was excited that the entire neighbourhood had been a witness to her vessels being carted away. Whenever she described that incident, her face lit up: 'They brought a bullock cart to transport the vessels!'

Amma retained two or three brass vessels, perhaps she still needed them. When she was living with us in Namakkal, my wife and I had to go to the village once. Amma asked us to bring back the brass vessels. 'It's yours. Why should it lie there anymore?' Without paying much attention to the details, we agreed and left.

Just as we were ready to leave, my wife remembered to bring down some of the brass vessels and carry it back home with us. Among them was a brass water pot. When we returned, Amma anxiously asked, 'Why did you bring this one? This is not yours.'

'Okay, Amma. I will take it back the next time I go there. Or if someone from Anna's family visits, we can give it to them,' I told her casually. My wife tried to console her by saying that we had brought it along accidentally. But Amma wasn't convinced. She was anxious, either at the thought that we were going to keep it, or that she was being unfair in her division of utensils between the two families.

The next day, the pot went missing from our living room and we were embarrassed to ask Amma about it. We found it two days later. She had placed it under the cupboard we kept our books in and had covered it securely with an old cloth. We didn't bring it up with her.

But I often wondered why she had hidden that brass pot. Fair division of property alone did not explain her behaviour. Unable to figure it out, I finally decided to ask her.

'Why have you kept that pot so carefully, Amma. Is it a golden pot?'

'Even though you have always lived with me, you have forgotten. Do you remember when that water pot was bought?'

Then came the background story.

When I was a young boy, the field we lived on had four to five wells for farming. As their water was saline, we fetched drinking water from the public well in the village, about half a mile from our home. Amma went to the well every alternate day to fetch water. She carried a brass cauldron on her head, atop a rolled piece of cloth to cushion the weight. The cauldron was so big that the water from it was sufficient for two days. When going to the well, she would carry some tamarind in her hand, because brass pots shone when cleaned with tamarind and soft water.

As the cauldron was big, neither Anna nor I could lift it, so only Amma could do this chore.

Once, she sprained her neck while carrying a sheaf of grass and couldn't carry the cauldron on her head to fetch water.

It would be difficult to carry the wide-mouthed cauldron on her hips. The water would spill over and her hands would ache after ten steps or so. Since we needed drinking water, Amma went to the well with mud pots on her hips.

An old woman who was drawing water from the well mocked my mother, 'Peruma! Don't you even have a brass pot? What have you earned from working all these days?'

Amma was deeply wounded by the jibe. From the next day, she started going to the well before dawn.

Soon enough, her sprain healed and she started fetching water in the brass cauldron during the day as usual. But she had made up her mind about something—she must buy a brass water pot. She sold one of our rams to the butcher, boarded a bus to the city right away and bought one.

A pot for the price of a goat, a pot that gave the old lady a fitting response, a pot that wiped off Amma's humiliation was surely a pot that needed to be cherished. Yes, it was indeed a golden pot.

20

# The Last Job

An abridged version of Amma's life would read: 'Work is life.' She worked all the time; that's all I ever saw her do. Even when recounting her childhood, she could only remember all the work she had done. Being a motherless child in a family caught in a financial crisis, Amma had to take on many chores. And after she married into an agrarian family, work became a way of life.

Farming demands rigorous toil, day and night. In the rain-fed agriculture that we practised, the work went beyond ploughing, sowing and harvesting. Rearing cattle was an important part of it.

We had a pen of goats and at least four or five cows and buffaloes. Taking care of them was a round-the-clock job.

Even if the other senses slowed down in the night when we were asleep, the ears had to stay alert. If a goat or a cow made the slightest noise, it was important to immediately check on it. The animal might have got tangled in the rope around its neck, it might be thirsty, snakes or wild cats might have got in or there could even be a thief. Amma woke up at the slightest of noises. I too caught the habit from her as time passed, and still wake easily.

If there was only farming to take care of, we could have travelled for a day or two, or visited a relative's home for a few days. But with goats and cattle, it was impossible to leave even for a few hours. If we did go, work piled up. We would also constantly worry about the animals and end up rushing back home. Amma hurried back even when she went to the market. Rain-fed agriculture is all about cultivating crops that can also be used as fodder for the animals. This meant that there was a lot of work even after harvest. Bringing the hay home and keeping it safe was quite a task.

There was no agricultural work that Amma did not know. She also helped out my father, and was familiar with all the work around the soda shop too.

A saying goes, 'Sleep after him and wake up before him,' to refer to an ideal wife who sees her husband as her god. This applies fully to women in agriculture. We never knew when Amma went to sleep or when she woke up. She was working when we went to sleep and working when we woke up. In fact, she woke us up only after finishing a few chores. On rare occasions, she took a half-hour nap during the day. Seeing her fast asleep filled me with fear; having always seen her busy at work, I worried that something had happened to her.

When Amma was bedridden for more than a year after her fall, her pace of work slowed. But she slowly recovered and resumed work.

She couldn't milk the buffaloes and sell them any more—a task she had done for many years. It was exhausting to care for milk-yielding buffaloes, so she only kept one calf at a time. She raised the calf and sold it when it became pregnant. Tending to the calf was relatively easy—tie it up with a long rope in the grazing field and give it some water once in a while. Sometimes, it needed to be retied in another spot. At night, it had to be fed once again.

When the calf got excited and ran around, it was difficult for Amma to catch hold of it, for which she needed as much strength as the calf. I worried that the calf might tug at the rope and Amma would fall down. Though I often told her to give up raising calves, she never listened. One day, just as I had feared, the calf tried to run, tugging at the rope. Amma let go of the rope to save herself. She sold the calf after this.

But she could not bear to remain idle and brought home a goat kid next. The goat kids we raised by hand at home, ran around our legs and stayed close to us. They needed to be tied up only after they grew up a bit. A pregnant goat that was full term sold for a good price. Amma would start with one goat. It would give birth to two or three kids, which she sold off once a year. The single goat eventually became three or four. Like this, Amma kept doing one thing or the other.

Could there be a dearth of work in the fields anyway? She picked up palm branches and fronds from under the tree and collected them for various uses. She cut and sold the wood from smaller trees. She ploughed and sowed using a tractor. She sold off what was sown even before the harvest.

There had always been a farmer in me, and twenty years ago, we tried to buy a plantation. A four-acre plot with two hundred coconut saplings came up for sale. But it was about six miles from our house.

'I'll go there and take care of it,' Amma reassured me.

I was hesitant.

'I won't be doing any work. I'll just stay there and supervise. I'll be fine,' Amma said firmly.

So it came to pass. I constructed a small house for Amma by the field. She handled the motor for the water, occasionally regulating the flow and making sure the saplings were watered.

Within a couple of months, she became familiar with the place and developed a bond with the neighbours. She blended and merged with this new environment. For nearly two years, she lived there all by herself, looking after the land. She was happy.

Circumstances forced us to sell the land. Amma returned to our village and continued to look after our rain-fed agricultural lands and our children. When I shifted to Namakkal with my family, the land and trees were enough for Amma.

Once, when I took her to a homeopathic doctor, I complained to him, 'Doctor, she doesn't rest up and is always running about.'

The doctor had been an army physician during the second world war. Although he was over ninety years old, he was healthy and still practising medicine. 'Why are you asking her to sit idle?' he asked. 'Let her do what she can. Why should anyone be idle? Life is movement, isn't it?'

His words were eye-opening. From then on, I never told Amma not to work. I only asked her to desist from work that would exhaust her, and warned her to be careful when working.

She didn't give up farming our land ever. It was never left fallow, and she always got hold of someone to do the sowing. Amma had a unique style of working: she finished the tasks that could be completed right away without a break and made long-term plans for those that required time. Nothing was ever postponed, not even the long-term tasks on which she spent fifteen to thirty minutes every day. If she missed doing it for a day, Amma would pick it up again the very next day. This is how she did so many tasks simultaneously.

One time, we noticed that a part of our field had many tiny stones, which does not augur well for farming. It is said that for every stone in the field, one plant will die. Amma had left four to five palm fronds in the land, and whenever she passed by that area, she swept some of the stones to one side. Once there was a heaped pile of stones, she emptied them outside the field. She did this for several years. One fine day, there were no stones left in the field.

Astonished at seeing the field, my grandmother said, 'The field was full of stones and you have removed them all by sweeping them up! There isn't a single stone now. Let's offer our prayers and apply the mud from the field on our foreheads as sacred ash.'

There were many such instances when Amma accomplished something little by little over a period of time. Even when she lived with us in Namakkal and was unwell, she always kept herself busy with some work around the house.

Her health was rapidly deteriorating and it was becoming difficult for Amma to use her limbs. We arranged a room for her on the terrace, and she spent her time between the room and the terrace.

Since the terrace floor had developed some cracks, we had to patch it up with cement. The labourers hadn't removed the cement splashed on the railings and it escaped our eyes. The three walls of the terrace too had cement splotches that looked like the footprints of an insect. One of Amma's visitors remarked that that the walls looked ugly because of the splotches.

By now, Amma was finding it difficult to eat. Parkinson's had crippled her hands and feet. She even struggled to pick up food in her hands and bring it to her mouth. Between mouthfuls of food, she needed to take breaks. It took her a long time to finish her meals.

'How long can I stay like this?' she would ask.

'Look outside. Look at the trees. There are sparrows flying. Look at them. Look at the sky. You can pass the time by looking at all these, Amma,' I would say.

But, for her, merely looking at something had no meaning. 'I could sit and watch all these things if I was a mad person like you. How can I merely look at something?'

Amma had seen endless varieties of birds on the field. She knew all the characteristics of trees, plants and creepers. I had learnt all about them from her. But she couldn't just look at them idly.

A metal brush used for scrubbing walls was lying around the terrace. Without my knowledge, Amma began scrubbing the cement off the walls. In the beginning, none of us knew what she was up to. When we found out by accident, one part of the wall was already clean, devoid of any cement splotches.

'What is this, Amma?'

She merely laughed.

Amma kept scrubbing the walls and cleaned them all little by little when we weren't around. It would have taken her three to four months. That was her last job.

21

# An Invisible Companionship

Amma passed away at 7.20 a.m. on 12 December 2012.

Born into an agrarian family as the younger daughter of Mari Gounder and Papayi in Sanarpalayam near Tiruchengode town, she was married to Perumal, son of landowning farmers Ramasamy and Paavayi, in Kootapalli, a mere three miles away. She was born into an ordinary family and lived the ordinary life of a struggling woman until the end. She suffered from Parkinson's for several years before being finally liberated from it—as if the sufferings she had endured all her life were not enough.

Unlike her death, one cannot be precise about her birth. It is difficult to even be approximate. I can only hazard a guess.

Amma would have been sixteen or seventeen years old at the time of her wedding. A year later, she was pregnant. Those were the days when it was not mandatory for women to go to a hospital for childbirth. A day after her water broke, the baby was yet to be born. Amma was not able to bear the pain any more. Taking pity on her, some people took her to the government hospital in Tiruchengode on a bullock cart. There, she gave birth to a stillborn boy—her first child, and a son at that. Amma somehow survived. She always felt, with a twinge of regret, that her son could have been saved had she reached the hospital on time. She never even got to see the child.

Two years later, my elder brother was born, and everyone who knew my parents thought he would be their only child. But I was born four years later. Amma was probably twenty-five years old when I was born. I am forty-seven years old now. Which means Amma would have been seventy-two if she were still alive. She must have been born in 1940 or 1941.

It is possible to identify the month of Amma's birth by her name: Perumayi. It was customary for people born in the month of Puratasi, mid-September to mid-October, to be given that name. My father was also born in the same month. He was named Perumal. Their compatibility went beyond their names; they were a loving couple.

Appa was an inveterate drunkard—and it took a toll on his health. Despite Amma's best efforts, she did not succeed in saving him. It has been twenty-five years since my father passed away. Since then, she remained independent and lived by herself. Amma's world revolved around her family—my elder brother and me. Our well-being has always been paramount to her, and she did everything to ensure our happiness.

Amma lost her mother before she was even old enough to remember. She had an elder sister. To some extent, the sisters enjoyed the love of their maternal grandmother. For some reason, my grandfather did not remarry. Appuchi rode a bullock cart that was used to transport heavy objects and was away a lot for several days at a stretch. My aunt and my mother grew up roaming around the countryside and playing with complete freedom. Their childhood was something that children today cannot even imagine. They swam in the village wells until their eyes turned red. Their hair was always dry and unkempt.

They played many games. Amma even knew how to play rummy! She played it with my kids too. There were many tricks she knew in the game of thayam—I have inherited her love for this game of dice, and have never been able to give up. For a game of thayam, I will drop everything and anything. When I played against Appa, it was Amma who taught me how to fling the dice.

Amma did not know to read or write. She never went to school, but had managed to figure out how to use numbers.

And also to read the calendar and tell time. Her mental arithmetic was exceptional. She kept track of income and expenditure unerringly.

To put an end to my mother's carefree days of running around the fields, Appuchi took her to an accountant's house in the city to work as a help there. She spent some years living there and a few travelling back and forth for her work there. Amma always said that the accountant and his family treated her well. She also said that, having been a motherless child, it was there that she learnt to take care of chores around the house. After this, she worked in restaurants, serving water at the tables. Amma, who had spent her youth living in the city, became a full-time village resident after her marriage.

She was the eldest daughter-in-law in a big farming family. She worked day and night in the fields and at home. My parents started an independent family in a separate house after I was born. Amma never spent an idle minute. She never procrastinated or palmed off work to someone else. As soon as she thought of something that needed doing, she had to complete the task. She managed cultivation, took care of the goats, cows and buffaloes. Since Appa ran a soda shop, he wasn't too keen on working in the fields. It was all left to Amma.

There was an accident in 1995. Amma was making a thatch out of groundnut creepers on a rock in our field, where we stored the fodder. She was an expert at making the protective covering that kept rain away. In order to weave the thatch, Amma stood on top, while my brother threw the creepers to her from below. Once she finished making the thatch, she spread out the palm leaves to complete the roof.

As she was climbing down, her leg slipped on a palm leaf and she fell headlong against the rock. Her back was badly hurt. She was bedridden for a month in the hospital, and remained in bed for another six months at home. With the strength of her mind alone, she recovered enough to resume her work within a year.

Amma knew everything, including how to irrigate, plough and drive a tractor. When I was young, I never saw my mother sleep. Amma was Movement itself.

I was my mother's boy. Shy and cowardly, I found my father's aggressive approach hard to adjust to. I liked my mother's warmth and love, and shared a cot with her till I was fifteen. I could sleep only if I curled up next to my mother's stomach, wrapped my legs around hers or hugged her tightly. Amma even had to accompany me when I went out to pee at night. When I was fifteen years old, Amma said to me, 'Now it's time for you to get used to sleeping by yourself.' She put out a separate cot for me right next to hers, and got me used to sleeping by myself.

I have thrown tantrums that I would go to school only if Amma accompanied me. She came with me to school, three miles away, and walked me back home every day. Though the boys made fun of me, I didn't want to let go of her. Then, she walked me from our house in the field only as far as the main road, and got me into the habit of going to school by myself. Amma stood on the road until I was no longer visible to her. I still treasure the memory of Amma standing on a road lined with tamarind trees, her gaze fixed on me.

She patiently taught me several things. I ran and hid at the very mention of swimming. My father once threw me into a well and I could not overcome the fear that I had felt that day. Amma instilled courage in me and took me to a well when no one was around. She gently taught me how to swim. In a few days, I was brave enough to swim with the help of a drumstick log. I then began to swim with others. Even then, Amma sat on the steps by the side of the well and kept an eye on me. This went on until I became a confident swimmer. When I think of her today, among the images of Amma etched in my mind is that of her sitting on her haunches by the well and gazing fondly at me.

It was Amma who also taught me how to cycle. Although I was nine years old, I was afraid of even the sight of a cycle, while all the boys my age already knew how to ride one. Anna learnt to cycle when he was six. My father, brother and other boys made fun of me. I felt like crying. Though Amma didn't know how to cycle, she could push one.

Back then, the Tiruchengode-Erode highway was deserted. A vehicle might pass by once an hour. In the afternoon and on moonlit nights, Amma held the bicycle, and I learnt to first pedal it and then jump on a moving cycle. I must be the only person to have learnt how to cycle without getting the smallest scratch. Amma's training was such. I have always felt her presence in everything I consider myself skilled in.

Bus travel did not agree with me. The odour of diesel made me nauseous. For my sake, Amma avoided buses and took to walking to wherever we had to go. When I was ten years old and had a fever, I refused to get on a bus. Amma carried me on her shoulders for five miles to the nearest hospital.

Every month, my father went to Palani on the day of the Krithikai star. Amma took several steps to avert my motion sickness—sending me on an empty stomach, giving me a lemon to smell when I felt nauseous, and suggesting that I spit on my hands and smell my saliva to keep the queasiness away—and sent me on those trips to Palani with Appa. She helped me get over my dislike of buses.

I also inherited Amma's way of thinking. She analysed everything intricately, examining an issue from various angles. Always fearful of the future, she worried that something untoward might happen. She weathered several tragedies in her life, saw many deaths and losses—the death of her mother, the absence of care from her father, the loss of her husband when she was only forty years old, the death of her first-born in her womb, the suicide of her elder son—triggered by debts at an age when he should have shouldered responsibilities, the loss of her house and lands, and a husband who squandered the family's earnings.

So she never slept soundly. She would wake up even at the slightest sound and scream 'Ah!' or 'Ayyo!'

'Why do you wake up like there's a fire, Amma?' I would ask her. However, my sleep and waking patterns are just like my mother's.

Amma didn't know how to destroy; creating came naturally to her. She left behind whatever she managed to create for our family. Amma did everything for us, ensuring that we never felt the absencc of a father. I will never stop feeling guilty about having sucked her blood dry during my higher studies. Wanting me to study without any worries, she hid many things from me. When she had to sell an ancestral property and a piece of land, she felt immense grief. She also struggled greatly to try and replace what we had lost.

She was always hesitant about new things, but tried to overcome this. When something was explained to her, she grasped it immediately. She was, for instance, afraid of the gas stove when it first came home. Once she understood how to operate it, she handled it with ease. When she was alone back in our village, I got her a cell phone. She learnt to use that too. She was very interested in radio, television and feature films. In fact, she had seen enough films to be able to identify actors and actresses. She was not very religious; occasionally, she prayed to our family deity, that was all.

Many boys who worked in the soda shop used to come home. So did my college friends, who also stayed over sometimes. After I became a college professor, many of my students too came home. As a result of this, Amma gave up the habit of being caste conscious. She never asked anyone about their caste identity. Always amicable, she never said anything to hurt a visitor. However, Amma never completely shed her caste consciousness. I witnessed the extent to which casteist beliefs exerted a hold on her subconscious mind when she lay dazed in her last days.

I was the only hope in Amma's life. So my marriage was a big blow to her. Mine was an inter-caste love marriage, and Amma refused to attend my wedding. She sold all her goats and cows and isolated herself in the house for several days. Yet, she offered to make a thali chain of seven sovereigns, to show that the we had the means to buy one; it was a matter of pride.

'You refuse to attend my wedding. Then why do you want to buy us a thali chain?' I refused her offer in strong terms.

My marriage was the only issue on which Amma and I had an open conflict. More than the fact that I was marrying outside our caste, she was afraid that I would move away from her.

She would have had many dreams about how to get me married—a woman from the same caste, from a rich family, an ostentatious wedding. When those dreams were shattered, she was afraid that her only hope was deserting her. I tried to tailor my behavior in order to dispel her fear.

So, she too began to be considerate with my family. Once again, she was my companion in all matters. Not even once did she tell me, 'Why did you get married like this?' She even visited my father-in-law's house. Had they lived closer, her relationship with my in-laws might have strengthened. She lavished the same love on my children as she did on my brother's. During her last days, I was astonished to see her being affectionate to my wife.

I have continued to feel Amma's eyes follow me everywhere—the eyes of a mother that follows a child who is learning to walk. When I was a toddler, I would first clutch Amma's hands and then shrug them off and walk on my own. I looked at her victoriously when I managed to walk, and sadly when I fell down.

Amma has always been my constant companion—she patted me encouragingly, lifted me up, hugged me and comforted me. That is how it is even today. An invisible companionship.

22

# A JOURNEY ALONG THE PATH OF THE WIND

Six months before Amma's death, we knew that she would leave us soon. I believed that she would live for a year at most. My relatives and friends who visited her felt the same. We only differed slightly in our estimation of how much longer she would be with us.

Even then, some people asked me, 'Where have you planned to keep her?' The question, common in these parts, is used to refer to both burial and cremation. 'He/She has been laid here,' people would say pointing to a spot. I found it difficult to respond immediately. There were ethical dilemmas here: I was hesitant to make that decision so soon, and I was uncomfortable talking about the death of someone who still lived. But there came a time when the decision had to be made.

I currently reside in the district headquarters. My birthplace, forty miles from here, is in the taluk headquarters. It wasn't a proper headquarters, only a village in the municipality.

People believe that, irrespective of where a person is when they die, their last rites should be conducted in their own village for their soul to rest in peace. This also makes it convenient for relatives to offer their condolences and take part in the rituals.

I have lost too many people—my maternal grandfather, paternal grandfather, father, paternal grandmother and my elder brother—in quick succession, perhaps too many for someone my age. We cremated Appuchi in our village. But we buried Thatha in our own land as per Appa's wish. When drunk, Appa was often found wailing at his father's burial spot, and he sometimes fell asleep there. Within a year of his father's death, Appa too passed away. People said that Thatha had taken him away since Appa had spent so much time at Thatha's place of burial. So we decided not to bury Appa in our land and took him to the village's cremation ground. It was also where Paati and Anna went. The cremation ground in the village was exclusive to the people of one caste.

Today, our village has progressed considerably. It is located within the municipality, and the advent of housing board colonies has led to the emergence of new localities, which eventually resulted in our village becoming part of the city. No one can say any more than our village is five miles from the city. Today, it is in the city. Since it is on the main road connecting two cities and since it has become a suitable residential area, our village has become a popular location.

If I were to tell someone which village I am from, they would immediately respond with, 'Oh, one of my relatives lives there ...'. It would be tough to explain what our old village used to be like, and so I would just say, 'Oh, is that so?'

Though there are no boundaries between our village and the city any longer, the village continues to retain two aspects of its individuality—the temple and the cremation ground. Protests by residents of the housing board colony and others have yielded no results. Under the Namakku Naame initiative, the crematorium now has a compound wall, a cremation platform and a memorial hall. To date it remains exclusive to the members of one caste.

My relatives wanted Amma to be taken there. There was no way we could be refused. I have regularly paid the temple tax for the annual festival in the village and so Amma was entitled to a spot in the cremation ground. Our house is on the border of another village, which too has a temple and a cremation ground. Since we pay tax to this temple as well, they couldn't refuse us a spot either.

I also own a house in the district headquarters where we live. It is in the suburbs and has been under a panchayat for a long time. After we relocated there in 2005, I came to know that people in the locality had asked a colleague of mine, who lived on our street, to find out about my caste. They had hoped that I wouldn't be a Dalit; any other caste was fine by them. My colleague too asked around in our college, but my caste identity wasn't easily discoverable.

Though my neighbours and I were from the same district, I wasn't from their region. I was new. I mingled with people from varied backgrounds and had no caste-based affiliations within the college teachers' association, so my colleague was unable to locate my caste. I usually hung around with Dalit students, so they suspected that I could be Dalit. But since they had no evidence yet, a professor who was adept at techniques of finding out about one's caste identity, set a trap for me.

He asked me if there were any suitable brides in my village for a boy in his family. Inevitably, we had to speak about caste.

It is the norm for the people of his caste to discuss clans when talking about marriage: People within a clan are not allowed to marry since they are considered to be paternal cousins. But people from other clans are deemed to be maternal uncles or brothers-in-law, and so marriage between clans is possible.

With this in mind, I asked my colleague which clan the boy belonged to. As the conversation progressed, I had to answer his questions—'Which clan do you belong to? Which temple do you belong to?'—and so I walked into the trap. He shut the door, locking me in the caste cage.

The news of his success reached my street. But my neighbours still had their doubts.

My wife wore a small nose pin with a single stone. It is not customary for people from the caste I was born into to wear a nose pin. Clothes, accessories, speech, physical traits and rituals are among the many ways in which a person's caste identity is ascertained. My wife's nose pin raised questions about ours.

Some, after confirming my identity, would say, 'But how come your wife wears a nose pin?' In our village, if a family lost babies one after another as soon as they were born, the nose of the next baby born would be pierced and she would be given the name 'Kuppayi'. I told some of them that my wife was one such child. But they didn't buy this story of mine.

They argued that, usually, such nose pins were removed later. The tiny hole on the nose might remain, but the women wouldn't continue to sport a nose pin. 'Only the "others" wear nose pins,' they told me. Many hesitated to socialise with us until they had some clarity. But, we were more or less accepted on our street. I came to understand first-hand how hurtful it would be for Dalits in such situations. Caste doesn't lose its hold even in urban suburbs. We got the approval of the street, and the problem of getting the village's approval remained.

This approval was determined by the two things I mentioned earlier—temple and cremation ground. Every year, in the Tamil month of Masi, mid-February to mid-March, around ten to fifteen people visit our street with a notebook in their hands, to collect tax for the annual temple festival. House owners have to pay a certain amount of tax, while tenants pay a lower amount. One way or the other, the tax has to be paid. I still don't know where the temple is, but I have been paying this tax for the last seven to eight years. Tax wasn't collected from Dalits, because that would give them rights and ownership. As in every village, there was a separate cremation ground for Dalits.

What if I don't pay? Apparently, we will then be denied access to the cremation ground. Here too, the cremation ground belonged to one caste. To gain access, one has to either be born into that particular community or in one of the other backward communities.

This cremation ground too, located on one side of a lake, was efficiently managed, like the one back in my village. Every time I pass the ground, I can't help but think that I pay tax because I need a place here. I had ensured a place in three villages by paying taxes to all of them. Amma had lived by herself in our village most of the time and spent only her last year with us.

When she and I were talking and the general mood seemed to be pleasant, I asked her half in jest, 'Where do we put you to rest, Amma?'

'Put it anywhere. A dead body can be on any street,' she said indifferently.

Amma knew that she had a place assured in three different cremation grounds. She had once asked me angrily why I was paying taxes in three villages.

'Okay. Tell me, which one do you want me to stop paying taxes to?' I asked her.

'We cannot afford to antagonise the people of our village. All right, it's meant for god. Go ahead and keep paying it. If I die tomorrow, you'd need a place in the cremation ground anyway.'

But I was sad that she hadn't picked any particular place. If people could decide on their place of rest themselves, it would solve many problems.

When the time to actually pick a place came, we gave it serious thought. Eventually, I decided on the district I was living in. That would make it convenient to conduct the death rituals. I had even considered donating Amma's body to a medical college. Both my father-in-law and mother-in-law had donated their bodies to a medical college. An organisation called Udavum Ullangal had taken the responsibility for transporting their bodies respectfully to the CMC Hospital in Vellore. Even my wife's relatives were satisfied with the way the organisation had handled it. But there was no such organisation here.

Rare books collector N.P. Ramasamy, who lives in the city, and his family, had declared through a written will that their bodies should be donated to the government medical college. Ayya's wife passed away a few months before my mother. No medical college made arrangements to transport her body. After difficult negotiations, the family took the body to the college. Ayya was deeply distressed by the institution's actions. On hearing this, I dropped the idea of donating Amma's body.

Though I regularly paid the temple tax, I couldn't bring myself to lay Amma in the cremation ground in our village. It was controlled by the members of a particular caste, and I would also have to stand in front of people I barely knew to seek permission. It would also be on my daily college commute route, and I would be reminded of Amma every day. So I decided against it.

The cremation ground that belongs to the municipality was common to all castes and communities. But it was filled with garbage and there was an open sewer nearby. No one who sees it would want to be laid there when they die.

We are plagued with problems when alive; why must death be so difficult too?

Even as I was occupied by these thoughts, a colleague's young son died of blood cancer. I went to attend the final rites of the professor's son, and saw an electric crematorium for the first time. It had just been set up and was well maintained, with trees and plants around. This was the ideal place to be after death, I thought. Finally, I decided on the electric crematorium for Amma—a public place that transcends castes and religions, and one where none can claim even six feet of land as theirs.

In an hour, the body is burnt and reduced to a handful of ash. It turns into smoke and dissolves into the atmosphere. This is how I sent off Amma, along the path of the wind. Amma, who has never known the outside world, will now witness and be enthralled by the vast expanse of the universe.

People who come to offer their condolences often ask, 'Where have you laid Amma to rest?'

I point to my chest. They laugh it off. No person or caste can claim rights over an electric crematorium. So if not my chest, where else was she laid to rest? Perhaps, I could point to space.